More Shelbydog Chronicles

More Shelbydog Chronicles

Reflections on a Dog's Life by Her Friend,
Knowing Your Pet

Mark G. Boyer

MORE SHELBYDOG CHRONICLES
Reflections on a Dog's Life by Her Friend, Knowing Your Pet

Resource Publications
An Imprint of Wipf and Stock Publishers
199 W. 8th Ave., Suite 3
Eugene, OR 97401

www.wipfandstock.com

PAPERBACK ISBN: 979-8-3852-0694-0
HARDCOVER ISBN: 979-8-3852-0695-7
EBOOK ISBN: 979-8-3852-0696-4

VERSION NUMBER 02/19/24

Dedicated to
Matthew Ver Miller,
one of Shelbydog's favorite friends,

and Jenson Kimmons,
Shelbydog's favorite bellyrubber!

Spiritual forces are inherent in humans, animals, and all natural phenomena.

—MARK NUTTALL, 131

Animals are spiritual beings endowed with souls. . . . [A]nimals must be propitiated and respected in order to ward off the vengeance of its soul.

—MARK NUTTALL, 132

Animals have a guardian, or master, who releases the animals in their care, only if people treat them with courtesy and respect.

—MARK NUTTALL, 132

. . . [E]verything in the world . . . has a life force and shares the same spiritual nature. . . . The Supreme Being is the personification of the life force which flows through and animates the human and animal worlds.

—MARK NUTTALL, 134

Contents

Contents

Introduction 1

I N MY PREVIOUS BOOK, *The Shelbydog Chronicles by Shelby Cole as Recorded by Mark G. Boyer: A Novel*, I narrated the adventures of my life from birth to age ten. Since that book was published by Wipf and Stock in 2022, I have not only aged, but a lot has happened to me. I have decided to present a follow-up volume now that I am preparing to celebrate my twelfth birthday; in human years that will make me 77 years old!—older than my friend, Mark, who has written this book. In this book, I've decided to let my friend, Mark, write about me. Of course, I will note every word he writes for its veracity.

Here is a summary about me. My name is Shelby Cole; I've kept the last name of my former owner, because he rescued me from a shelter after I had spent the fifth year of my life in shelters. After he and his wife decided to move to Florida, I went to live with Mark, because I do not handle the heat and humidity well. I had spent a lot of time at Mark's house, and he was more than willing to keep me out of Florida. In fact, when asked by my former owner how he intended to deal with me, he told my former owner that he was going to love me. And that is exactly what he has done. What the chapters in this book will demonstrate is how much he has loved me.

My mother was a Labrador and my father was a Boxer. I was born April 7, 2012, in a kennel. I had four brothers and one sister; I have never seen them again. When we were two months old, we were taken to a pet store to be sold. Because my brothers and sister displayed fur in various designs of black and white, they were purchased first. Because I was brindle—brown with streaks of dark cream and red highlights—I was not the usual color a dog was supposed to be. Nevertheless, I was purchased by Robert and Susan, taken to their home, and either neglected—not fed and watered—or punished for being me or not doing what they wanted me to do or to be. I was left outside in the elements, and that made me afraid of thunder and lighting. I was kicked. I was beaten with a stick. I was sprayed with a hose. I was an explorer and an escape artist! I grew to weigh sixty pounds. But I was not the dog Robert and Susan wanted. They wanted a dumb dog, but they got me, a smart dog. The first four years of my life were miserable. When Robert and Susan decided to move, they took me to a shelter, because they didn't want to take me with them. They had tried everything they knew to use to discipline me—except love. I spent the fifth year of my life in shelters. Finally, I was adopted by Mark's friend, Corbin, who introduced me to Mark; Mark became my companion. He got to know me, and that is why he is writing this book about me.

If you would like to get to know more about me, please purchase a copy of *The Shelbydog Chronicles by Shelby Cole as Recorded by Mark G. Boyer: A Novel.*

Shelby Cole
November 1, 2023

Introduction 2

WITH SHELBYDOG'S PERMISSION, I will share the experiences I have had with Shelby over the past four years. She entered my home and my life, and caused chaos, which has resulted in change for me. In other words, she has made me a better person. She has taught me compassion, altruism, love, and more. Shelby has taught me the importance of praising her for doing what I want and to gently discipline her when she does something I told her not to do. Since Shelby came to live with me, my life revolves around her; she is the center of my life.

Five years ago, my friend, Corbin, chose Shelby from several other dogs at the local shelter. He told me that he made several trips to the shelter to view the dogs available and, as it were, interview them. As he narrowed the candidates, Shelbydog stood out to him. So, after learning about her, spending time with her, walking her, and talking to her and observing how she responded to him, he decided to choose her. Since she had spent the fifth year of her life in shelters, I don't know what would have happened to her if he had not chosen to take her home with him.

I'm offering the following reflections on Shelbydog's life and how it intersects with mine in the hope that you, the reader, will do your own reflecting on your pet and become more aware of how your life intersects with your pet's life. The chapters that follow are in no particular order; they attempt to capture in words the dog I have been privileged to know and love for four years. At the end of each chapter there are reflection questions that will, hopefully, help you get to know your pet better. Shelby has required a definite commitment from me of time, development of talent, and use of treasure in her care. I spend time walking her and feeding her, petting her and giving her bellyrubs, covering her with her blanket and re-covering her during the night. Her needs come before mine, as I give her her daily medicine and care. When needed, I take her to her veterinarian. Her food, medicine, and vet costs are paid out of my treasure. She has changed my life from morning to evening and even through the night.

I am aware of her aging; we take shorter walks than we used to take; she has slowed her pace during walks; she sleeps more during the day. Because of her aging and, ultimate, passing from this life, I have been grieving. I read a book on preparing for a pet's death (*When It's Time to Say Goodbye: Preparing for the Transition of Your Beloved Pet* by Angela Garner, Findhorn, 2021), and that book has helped me face and plan for the inevitable future. Watching online videos about dogs dying and researching arrangements in pet cemeteries makes me sad, as my life revolves around Shelbydog—three daily feedings, three daily walks, many pettings and bellyrubs, and rides in my car on errands. I know that my life will change again when she dies. However, I have made a promise to her that when the time comes, I will bury her with dignity and I will provide a marker for her. While I hope I don't have to do this soon, I know that in a few years I will be faced with her death. Because we know each other so well, we share our life breath with each other, and, in so doing, fill each other with divine grace. Shelby possesses a spirituality, as I note in chapter 20 below. She is my burning bush in animal form.

Since I usually get out of bed long before Shelby does, when she does awaken and get up, I stop what I am doing to take her on a walk and, then, feed her. I stop at lunchtime to feed her, and then take her for a post-lunch walk; if the weather is too hot, I take her to the back yard so she can pee and/or poop. In the dark days of winter, I stop what I am doing at 4 p.m. to take her for a walk before it gets dark, then I feed her dinner. My life revolves around Shelby, my burning bush, the manifestation of the divine in my life and home.

As we become more and more transparent to each other, Shelby has made it a point to get both physically and spiritually closer to me. She visits me wherever I am in my home. She cooperates more and more in taking her medicine and eating all the food in her bowl. She thinks that she has stolen my heart—which she has!—and can do whatever she wants. Frequently, I tell her, "I get to decide some things, like the route we will walk." However, when she comes to me without being called and lies on her back with all four feet in the air, I cannot resist giving her the bellyrub she is requesting. In other words, she has grown in confidence that she can get what she wants from me! And I have grown in confidence that I can meet her needs.

When Shelbydog first came to live with me, I knew nothing about dogs or their care. I mentioned that to her veterinarian, when I took her to her first vet appointment. Her vet told me that she would help me, and she has. There has been nothing I cannot talk about to her vet or e-mail her and get an answer.

When it is not too hot and we can take a post-lunch walk to the garden a few blocks away, my favorite part of that walk is Shelby's sitting on the stone bench, or, when the sun is shining on it, sitting on the picnic table, while I give her a drink of water and pet her and talk to her and tell her how much I love her. Usually, she responds by licking my hand, that is, giving me Shelbydog kisses! After a short rest, I lift her off the bench or table, place her on the ground, and we continue our walk. She is a wonderful companion. She is a dog I am proud to know.

Mark G. Boyer
November 1, 2023

1

The Promise

WHEN SHELBY CAME TO live with me occasionally, she had a rap sheet. Not only had she bitten her first owners, but she had a habit of nipping people (for example, pants' leg), when they did not give her the attention she thought was due her. She had also destroyed her wire kennel twice, chewed on a door, demolished a plastic storage container, dug a large hole in my back yard, and learned to climb the chain-linked fence in order to get out of the yard. Thus, the evening when Corbin told me that he was going to leave her with me, when he and his wife moved to Florida, he asked me, "What are you going to do with her?" My response to him was this: "I am going to love her."

I think I caught him off guard, because he looked at me with a question on his face. I told him that I had already promised Shelbydog that if she stayed with me, that I was going to love her, even as I was going to get to know her better. While I had gotten to know her well over the past few years, I still had a lot to learn. I was determined to show her respect in the hope that she would return it to me. As a result, the more I loved her, the more responsive she became to me. The more respect I showed her, the more she showed to me. The more I talked to her, the more she talked to me. Yes, there were times when it was very frustrating, because we fell into a contest of wills. But through it all, I loved her, and the changes that took place in her continue to this day.

Reflection Questions

1. How well do you know your pet?

2. Do you love your pet? Explain.

3. What change(s) has (have) your pet caused in you?

4. What promise(s) have you made to your pet?

2

Walks

T HE BEST WAY I got to know Shelby was taking her on walks. When she was younger, we would take a two-mile walk in the afternoon with a short trip to the backyard after she got up and another before she went to bed. Once it got too hot for her in the afternoon, we changed our routine to a mile walk after she got up in the morning, either a short after-lunch walk or a trip to the backyard, and a short after-dinner walk in the summertime evening or a late afternoon, before-dinner walk in the winter.

Now that Shelby is over eleven years old, we have had to adjust our walking schedule even more. Even in the early summer mornings, we walk four blocks down the street and back. When it is hot, we go to the back yard after lunch, and walk only one square block after the sun goes down behind the trees. In other words, those two-mile afternoon walks have been replaced with several shorter walks. Of course I carry water with us on all walks, and we stop frequently for Shelby to get a drink and to take a break for a few minutes. On warm days, she will take the short way home; she knows all the side streets!

On warm days after lunch, Shelby likes to walk to a flower garden two blocks away. On the way there, she stops under trees in the shade to rest. When we get to the garden's entrance, she has her favorite paths to take to a stone bench, upon which she likes to lie for a rest, while I give her a drink and pet her. When the sun is shining on the bench, we go to a picnic table, upon which she jumps from the bench to the top of the table and lies upon it for a rest, while I give her a drink of water. She used to drink out of my left hand, as I poured water from a bottle with my right hand. However, she likes drinking from the bottle with a trough attached that my neighbor gave her.

On our walks, I have learned that Shelby likes to walk. Often, she will begin pestering me before a usual time for a walk by finding me and placing one of her front paws on my knee. At other times, she will follow me through the house waiting for me to say, "Are you ready for a walk?" If I pick up her leash or a poop bag or put on my jacket or coat, she reads those signs and gets excited—running through the house—about going on a walk. Sometimes before a walk I will see her sitting in a doorway and peering around the door frame to see if I am on my way toward the front door. When she sees me, she hunkers down—front feet and head on the floor with back feet and butt in the air—wagging her tail and listening intently for the sounds accompanying a walk, like the tearing of poop bags off a roll, the rattling of her leash, or the swish of putting on a jacket. When she is sure that a walk is imminent, she runs to the front door.

On our walks, she stops frequently to smell tree roots and bushes, where she often pees. She looks for grass in yards and street grass islands, where she poops. By her pace and stride, I know when she is looking for a place to poop. When she has finished pooping, she begins to trot; I hold her leash while putting a green waste bag over my hand, picking up her poop, tying a knot in the plastic bag, holding on to its top, and continuing our way. Often, the trot turns into a run for a few feet.

Shelby will not let just anyone walk her; she is very particular. She will not go for a walk with my neighbors, who have tried to take her when I have been sick. They can hold the leash, but I have to go along. She will walk with some of my friends, but not all of them, without me accompanying them. The people with whom she will walk without me are those she has gotten to know very well by spending time with them; they are her friends. I do not know what are the criteria for judgment she uses to trust them to take her on a walk.

She does not like to walk in the rain, even if there are only a few raindrops. For very light sprinkles, I put on her coat so she cannot feel the raindrops. If she feels a single drop, she turns around abruptly and heads back home. Sometimes when the rain has stopped and we go outside for a walk, she feels the damp sidewalk under her paws and thinks it is raining or going to rain, and turns around and heads toward home!

On trips to Colorado, Shelby likes to walk trails in the forests. She used to have to be in the lead, when others joined us for a hike. Now, she is content to be at the end of the line of hikers. As long as we stop periodically for a brief rest, she is ready to hike the next part of the trail. I keep her off scree, because she does not know how to place all four of her feet on it and I fear that she will get a leg stuck in the rocks or break a leg. After a hike, Shelby needs a couple of days to recuperate.

As Shelby gets older, she slows down more and more on walks. If she is hot, she dawdles, looking for shade, rolling, resting, getting a drink. On our long morning walk, she begins to wear out two or three blocks from home, and when we get home, she wastes no time lying on her pallet as soon as I open the door to the front porch. After resting for a few minutes, she will get up, get a drink of water, and come to the kitchen to get her breakfast.

Shelby likes to decide the route we will take on our walks, although she has a tendency to pick the same route for morning, noon, and evening. She is a creature of habit and routine. When I attempt to alter the usual walking way, she doesn't like it. However, when it is very hot, I have to cut short a walk to keep Shelby from getting too hot.

Reflection Questions

1. What activity has helped you the most to know your pet?

2. Who can walk your pet? Make a list. Who cannot walk your pet. Make a list. Why not?

3. Does your pet like to walk in the rain? Explain.

4. What effect does age have on your pet?

3

Joints (Limitations)

S INCE SHELBYDOG CAME TO live with me, she has had joint issues. During her sixth year of life, I was walking her one morning. She stopped suddenly, unable to move. No matter what I tried, she could not move. So, I had to pick up this sixty-pound dog and carry her back to my house. We were but a few blocks away. After putting my arms under her belly and lifting her, I'd walk a half a block, and I would have to put her down. After a short rest, I'd pick up Shelby again and walk another half a block.

Finally, after repeating this process over and over, we got back home. I carried her up the steps and put her down on the front porch. Then, I called Corbin, her then-owner, and told him what had happened. He called Shelby's veterinarian, who told him to buy Cosequin and begin to give it to her. I prepared a pallet for her to lie upon on the front porch. Later that day Corbin brought the Cosequin, which she began to take every day for joint improvement.

During the summer of 2022, I noticed that the slight limp she had on the front left leg was getting worse, especially after she stopped one morning and couldn't move. I waited with her for a while, then we walked a short distance, stopped, and continued until we got home. I had noticed that Shelby had stopped trotting and running. I called her vet and got an appointment in a few days. After examining her, the vet determined that she had some joint inflammation. Then, she presented options for Shelbydog's health. I chose a drug called Carprofen, which eliminated any joint inflammation; I saw improvement the next day with the return of trotting and running.

She took Carprofen twice a day for a week, then once a day after that. I also chose an advanced form of Dasuquin, a daily restorative chew. During the summer of 2023, Shelby's limp got worse. So, I began giving her Carprofen twice a day and the regular form of Dasuquin once a day in addition to the advanced form. After investigating shoulder braces, I got her a double front shoulder brace, which she began to wear on walks. Even though Shelby likes to wear things, at first, she didn't know how to let the double-shoulder brace help her. After a few walks, I noticed that she began to let it support her front legs and feet. And with it on, she began to trot and run again.

It was right after our daily use of the shoulder brace that I went online to figure Shelby's dog years into human years. I discovered that both of us were the same age. Since I was in touch with my limitations, knowing that she was the same age as I made me aware of her limitations. We began to shorten our daily walks and to omit the post-lunch walk on hot days, because Shelby does not like the heat. We got our early morning four-block walk in before it began to warm up, went to the back yard after lunch, and waited until the sun sat behind the trees to take our two-block evening walk or one-block evening walk, if it was still very hot. I always put on her double-shoulder brace, and that assisted her movement.

Reflection Questions

1. What issues does your pet have? What limitations do those issues impose upon your pet?

2. In what specific ways have you (or your pet's veterinarian) addressed your pet's issues?

4

Bellyrubs

S HELBY HAS AN UNCANNY ability to turn any type of petting into an occasion for a bellyrub. In the morning I will be working in my office, and she will come to check on me. She will sit by my office chair, and I will pet her head and talk to her. After a few strokes, she will lie on the floor, first on her belly and then on her side. That means she wants a bellyrub.

In the afternoon, when I sit down to read, she comes to the living room and lies on the rug. Then, she rolls over onto her back and puts all four feet up into the air. The front feet bend down slightly at the ankles. She will stay in that position until I get out of my chair and sit on the floor beside her and give her a bellyrub. While getting the bellyrub, she remains on her back sometimes and rolls to her side at other times. After a while of getting a bellyrub, she stands up, shakes herself, and leaves.

She does the same thing when others come to visit. During conversation, she goes to the other person or to me and, after lying down, rolls onto her back with all four feet in the air requesting a bellyrub. After getting a bellyrub, she may request more by rolling on her back if she has rolled onto her side or merely staying in her bellyrub position.

If I awaken her, on most mornings, while still in her bed, she rolls onto her back with all four feet up in the air requesting a bellyrub before she gets up and goes for a walk. Likewise, when we travel and sleep in a queen-size or king-size bed, before she gets up she rolls onto her back requesting a bellyrub from me!

When we visit friends, the people she likes the best are often solicited for a bellyrub at some time during the visit. I point to her lying on her back with all four feet in the air and ask, "What do you think she wants?" She is an expert at requesting and getting bellyrubs.

Reflection Questions

1. What is your pet's favorite way to get attention (petted)? During the day, how often does your pet seek attention (to be petted)?

2. How does your pet respond to visitors?

5

Play

W HILE SHELBYDOG ENJOYS BEING a solitary, she also enjoys solitary play. One of her favorite ways to play is to throw herself onto a rug, roll over on her back with all four feet in the air, and wiggle. She moves her head and upper torso one way and the rest of her body the opposite way. It looks like she is scratching her back. Sometimes, she rolls over and over again and then back. On walks, she has her favorite places in the grass for rolling and wiggling. After a few minutes of rolling and wiggling—no matter where—she stands up, shakes herself from nose to tail, and either returns to the front porch or continues the walk. When she has on her leach, I have to move it in rhythm with the rolling so that she does not get tangled in it or it gets wrapped around one of her legs.

She also likes to play with a bed pillow she has in the living room. While sitting in front of the pillow and breathing heavily, with her front feet she rolls it up under herself and tosses it in a direction she chooses. Then, she walks over to it, sits down in front of it, and, while breathing heavily, rolls it up under herself until she tosses it aside again. When she is tired of playing with the pillow, she lets it lie where it landed and goes back to the front porch.

While she has a box full of toys, she plays with only a few of them. She does not like to play with a ball. She does like to play with her duck. She takes duckie out of her toy box and lies on the floor with duckie secured in her front paws, while she licks duckie from bill to tail. She has never torn duckie. In fact, she has a travel duckie, too. When someone appears at the front door—such as the FedEx carrier, UPS carrier, or postal carrier—she picks up duckie and brings it to the front door to share her toy with the person at the door. I instruct them, saying, "Take duckie from her and then give it back immediately." If the person does that, Shelby brings duckie to the door, shares it, receives it, and returns to her place on the porch.

She owns a brown deer, called deerie. Just like she takes duckie and cleans it from bill to tail, she also takes deerie out of her toy box, carries it to the front porch, and proceeds to clean it from antlers to tail. If she cannot find duckie—because she carried it somewhere into the house—she picks up deerie and brings it to the door. Before I open the glass door, I tell the person on the other side that she will not hurt him or her, and I give instructions what to do: "Take deerie from her and then give it back. That is all there is to it."

A third toy Shelby likes to share with visitors is a cloth rectangle. When she cannot find either duckie or deerie, she will get the rectangle and bring it to the front door to share with a guest.

For her eleventh birthday in 2023, a young boy—named Jenson—who lives a few blocks down the street, brough her a cloth bone with "It wasn't me" printed on it. She takes it out of her toy box and brings it to the front porch from time to time.

She never destroys duckie, deerie, the rectangle, or the cloth bone Jenson gave her. Her favorite toy to rip into pieces is a cloth bone filled with stuffing and a squeaky toy. She will play with the cloth bone for hours, locating the thread stitching and pulling it out piece by piece. Then, she removes the stuffing, taking it out piece by piece and piling it on either side of her head. Once she finds the squeaky inside, she removes it and places it in one of the piles of stuffing. She may continue to play with the cloth bone or save it for another day, when she will remove more of the stuffing.

Reflection Questions

1. How does your pet play? Explain.
2. With what items does your pet play?

6

Cat Mode

After carefully watching a cat clean its front paws and wash its face, Shelby adopted a process I refer to as entering cat mode. Especially after being outside for a walk, she will lie on a rug in the house and lick her paws clean. After she moistens her paws, she will pass them over her face to wash her face—her head, eyes, ears, and nose; she may do this several times, until she has assured herself that her face is clean. Then, she may wash her paws again.

Shelby does not like cats. To her a cat is supposed to run away. And that is exactly what cats we see on neighborhood walks do. They may sit and watch us coming from afar, but when we get close, they run and hide.

However, the cat who lives next door was raised with a dog. Hence, that cat is not scared of dogs, and Shelby does not know what to do when that cat is near her. Two times, while speaking with the cat's owner, the cat, Vera, has emerged, walked to Shelby, and licked her nose. Shelby was paralyzed in place. She did not know what to do or how to respond. A cat is supposed to run away in fear; Vera invades Shelby's personal space. After a minute or so, Shelby stood and moved away from Vera. Sometimes, Shelby begins to head toward home. If she sees Vera in the driveway, Shelby goes around her, as far away as possible. I find it interesting that Shelby imitates the creature she likes to chase!

In addition to washing her feet, paws, and face like a cat, Shelby often growls for a long time in imitation of how a cat purrs. While it is a guttural growl—not a bark—to Shelby it sounds like a cat purring. Shelby's purring may go on for a minute or more. Such is Shelby's behavior when she enters cat mode several times a day!

Reflection Questions

1. Does your pet like cats? Explain.
2. Does your pet imitate cats? Explain.

7

Cow Mode

AFTER OBSERVING COWS BEFORE she came to live with me, Shelby has adopted what I refer to as cow mode. First, she likes to speak in the same way that cows often cry to each other. Even though cows are much larger than she is, she will stop and stare at them for the longest time, while the cows stare back. Neither makes a move. If the cow has a calf, it will call the calf closer; Shelby will growl like a cow.

Second, Shelby thinks that cow manure smells good. So, if she can find a cow patty of fresh cow manure, she will fall on her back and roll in it. She will stand up and throw herself down onto it with her head and neck landing on it. Then, more roling and wiggling follow, as she spreads it all over herself. As soon as she gets home, of course, she has to have a bath. What she thinks smells good is not shared by the human population!

Similarly, one day while walking to a favorite garden, she found human feces; some homeless people had spent the night in the gazebo in the garden and left their poop in the garden. While I was observing a blooming flower, Shelby found the human feces and rolled in it, spreading it all over her head and back. I had to take her home and give her a bath.

Reflection Questions

1. Does your pet like cows? Explain.

2. Does your pet imitate cows? Explain.

8

Bed (Sleep)

I N GENERAL, SHELBY SLEEPS in her own bed, located next to mine, which has a bolster on three sides of it. Usually, she places her head on a bolster, sometimes with her front paws under her head, and sleeps. When we go to bed, I cover her from nose to tail with a blanket, as that is her favorite way to sleep. During the night, she changes positions; sometimes she lies on her side, other times she curls in a ball, and still other times she stretches out over the length of her bed. If she wiggles her way out from under her blanket, she will awaken me with a paw placed gently on my bed. I will lean over, find her blanket, and re-cover her. Within a few minutes I will hear her snoring again.

After she came to live with me, I bought a dog bed for Shelby. At first, I had made a pallet for her out of rugs and an old quilt, then I decided to buy her a bed. Her first bed was dark brown on the outside and cream on the inside. It featured a bolster all around with about two inches of inner padding. The stuffing gradually flattened, and Shelby began to scratch the bottom in an attempt to fluff it. I put an old pillow on the inside, and she slept on that until I purchased her a new bed.

Her new bed was larger, featuring dark blue on the outside and light blue on the inside. A bolster covered three sides. The stuffing in the bolsters could be removed along with the bottom or inside padding so that the shell could be washed. While the bolsters remained fluffed, the bottom padding flattened. In 2020, I removed all padding, washed the shell, replaced the bolster padding, and replaced the bottom padding with two layers of memory foam. By 2022, Shelby had broken the top layer of memory foam under the bottom shell into tiny pieces that had been coming out of the bed and spreading all over the floor. Before going to bed at night, she liked to scratch her bed; thus, a few small holes had appeared in the bottom of her bed.

After removing all the memory foam and the bolster stuffing, I washed the shell. Then, I cut two pieces of denim the size of the bottom and sowed one piece on the top of the bottom and one piece under the bottom. That made the bottom stiff, and Shelby was not able to scratch a hole in it.

After replacing the bolster stuffing, I placed a blanket in the bottom of the bed with the remaining sheet of intact memory foam behind it. Then, I zipped it closed. The first night she got into it she realized that the denim made it stiff, and she began to scratch it. So, I told her, "Do not scratch your bed." I had to say that a few more times in subsequent days, but after a few weeks she had stopped.

When traveling thereafter, I was bringing her old bed with us so she had a bed in which to sleep. One night she observed the queen bed in our motel room. As we were getting ready to go to bed, she jumped onto the queen-size bed and lay on a lower portion of it. While I told her to get into her bed, she would not move. So, I covered her with her blanket, and we slept next to each other that night. Now, anytime we travel and there is a queen- or king-size bed in our motel room, she makes it a point to jump onto it and sleep on one side. Sometimes the beds are very high, and Shelby, in her older years, is not able to jump onto them. In that case, I pick her up and put her on the bed. In the morning, I pick her up off the bed and put her on the floor, as I don't want her jumping from that height and further hurting her joints.

One day in the spring of 2022, I was cleaning our bedroom. In order to mop the floor, I picked up Shelby's bed and put it on my bed. She came into the bedroom, saw that her bed was gone, and looked at me with the saddest face. I told her that I would put it back as soon as I had cleaned the floor upon which her bed rested. After mopping the area, I put back her bed in its place, called her, and she came and investigated it. A smile appeared on her face as she lay in it.

Once when traveling, after she had jumped onto the bed, I went to the bathroom to brush my teeth. When I re-entered the room, there was Shelby in my place on the bed with her head resting on my pillow. After laughing out loud at her rascal move, I made her move over to her side of the bed.

After we change from standard time to daylight savings time in March, Shelby will often fall asleep on a rug on the front porch, where she likes to sit and watch car lights pass by. When I am ready to go to bed, I awaken her and tell her it is time for bed. I often pet her gently on the head and back and tell her, "It's time to go to bed." She awakens and I move to the door. I keep calling her to get up and come to bed. It usually takes four or five calls, a whistle, and the use of the word *now* to get her moving. Once she arises, she heads for the bedroom, where I put her to bed.

When the time change occurs from daylight savings time back to standard time in November, after she has eaten her dinner, she spends a short amount of time on the front porch. It is not uncommon to watch her head to her bed around 5:30 or 6 p.m. I follow her, pray with her, kiss her on the head, cover her with her blanket, and she sleeps until the next morning. In the late fall, all winter, and early spring, Shelby sleeps from twelve to fifteen hours a day!

While it is not a common occurrence, in the dark days of the winter she may fall asleep on a pallet she has on the front porch. When that happens, I cover her with a blanket until I am ready to go to bed. I have often commented that she looks very innocent and sweet lying on her pallet, and she stirs all kinds of love in me, until I awaken her to get up and come to her bed.

During the short days of the winter, it is not unusual for her to sleep until 8 or 9 a.m. After she gets up, I put on her harness, shoulder braces, and bandana, and we go outside for a walk no matter how cold it may be; if it is very cold, I also put her coat on her. At times, I need her to get up earlier because I need to keep an appointment. When I get her out of bed earlier, I pet her and talk to her, urging her to get up. Usually, I give her a bellyrub, then walk away while continuing to call her to arise. After a few minutes, I hear her getting up and heading my direction. During the longer days of the summer, her circadian rhythm kicks in, and she gets up with sunrise, sometime between 5:00 and 6:30 a.m. Often, she will awaken me with a paw on my bed, when she sees the light streaming through the window. Then, after I get up, I get her ready for our morning walk, and off we go.

For the month of August in 2022, I rented an apartment in Colorado that had a queen-size bed in it. Every night Shelby would jump onto it and sleep near me. I'd cover her with her blanket, and, because she moved around a lot during the night, I'd have to re-cover her two or three times. After I'd get up in the morning, she would remain in bed until I got dressed and was ready to begin the new day. Then, she would jump off the bed, and I'd get her ready for her morning walk.

By August 2023, Shelby's joint issues had worsened. While she could still jump onto the bed, I didn't want her jumping off the bed and hurting her shoulders; in the morning, I lifted her off the bed and placed her on the floor. So, for a few nights she slept near me. But then she became restless. So, I retrieved her old bed from the car, prepared it by my bed, and insisted that she sleep in her own bed. While she was reluctant to do so at first, she gradually accommodated herself to sleeping in her own bed, from which she could get up at night to get a drink or to investigate a sound she may have heard.

At home, Shelby usually sleeps through the night. From about October through March, she may get up and stretch during the night, but returns to bed, and I re-cover her with her blanket. From March through October, we run a window air conditioner to keep our bedroom very cool. The white noise of the air conditioning unit drowns any outdoor noises, and Shelby sleeps all through the night.

Because there is no white noise in our Colorado apartment and the windows are open, Shelby hears all the noises of the night, and, being the curious and nosey dog that she is, gets up to investigate them.

As Shelbydog ages, I find myself appreciating the gift that she has been to me. I hug her often during the day. I kiss her goodnight on her head. I tell her that I love her. I pray with her before covering her with her blanket in the evening or at night. She has caused great change in my life that has brought about growth in me.

Reflection Questions

1. Where does your pet sleep?

2. In what positions does your pet like to sleep? Explain.

3. Does your pet have his or her own bed? Explain.

4. Does your pet sleep with you? What are the pros and cons of that arrangement?

5. What growth has your pet sparked in you? Explain.

9

Favorite Places

O NE OF SHELBY'S FAVORITE places is the garden two blocks away from where we live. The garden is a project of city utilities, the park's department, and Master Gardeners. In the flower garden is a stone bench, upon which Shelby likes to jump and sit while I give her a drink from her water bottle. There is also a picnic table in the shade; when the sun is hot, we go to the picnic table. Before she began wearing her shoulder braces, she used to jump onto the seat and then onto the table, where she would lie with her front feet hanging off the edge, while I gave her a drink of water. With her double shoulder brace on, she is not able to jump onto the table; thus, I lift her up and place her on it. I always lift her off the table so that she is not jumping and further injuring her joints.

Another favorite place Shelby likes to visit is the Montessori School located near the garden. One group of students in the playground adopted her during the spring of 2023. Their teacher used the occasion to teach them about dogs. The teacher opened the playground gate and five or six students came out calling Shelby by name. They petted her and gave her bellyrubs. I brought kibble with me one time, and gave each of them a kibble so they could feel Shelby's rough tongue on their hands. After school was over in May, Shelby kept looking for the students, when we passed by the playground.

Shelby likes her back yard, where she strolls around the walkways after going to her favorite grassy spot to pee. She investigates every corner of the fenced-in yard. Once she has done that, she is ready to return to the house.

If I am working in the front yard or doing something in the garage, Shelby likes the front yard. She has a favorite grassy spot, where she lies in the sun until she gets too hot. Then, she moves to the shade on the driveway or into the garage.

Inside the house, Shelby's favorite place is the front porch; that is her room. After she gets up in the morning, she heads for the glass door to see what is going on outside. When we return from walks, that is where she stays; she has a water bowl there with fresh water put into it daily. She lies in the sun there in the morning, sleeps there in the afternoon, and falls asleep there in the evening. There, she barks at delivery people, her favorite postal carriers, and anyone else who approaches the front door or steers a car onto the concrete driveway. Sometimes she even eats her meals there.

The back seat of my Jeep is another of Shelby's favorite places. If she notices that I am getting ready to leave, she finds me and asks—using her body posture—if she can go. If she doesn't notice, she hears my Jeep keys jingle, and she heads to the door from the house to the garage. I used to have to ask, "Do you want to go for a ride?" but I need not do that anymore. If for some reason I need to move the Jeep out of the garage, Shelby will often get into the back seat, while I back it out of the garage. She has been known to stay in the back seat even after I have exited the Jeep and left the car door open so she can get out!

Reflection Question

1. Where are your pet's favorite places? Make a list, and identify why each is a favorite place.

10

Medicines

WITHIN THE FIRST YEAR that Shelbydog came to live with me, I mentioned her sensitive skin to her veterinarian. I explained how she spent a lot of time scratching herself, even though there was no reason (no tick, flea, or sore) to do so. Her vet prescribed Apoquel. That daily one-half of a pill brought the unnecessary scratching to an end within a few days. During the summer, when Shelby's skin dries more, I often have to give her a dose in the morning and in the afternoon or evening to alleviate the scratching.

In addition to the Apoquel, I found a skin-sensitive shampoo, called Dog Wash, which I use when giving her a bath. It doesn't dry her skin, like many other shampoos do.

At the same time as the veterinarian prescribed Apoquel, I mentioned that Shelby snored and that she often awakened with lots of crusty stuff in her eyes, which I removed with a wash cloth soaked in hot water. The vet told me to give her a daily Claritin, which would help with those alergies. Now, from April through October, Claritin controls Shelby's allergies.

Once the vet determined that Shelby had some joint inflammation, she prescribed Carprofen (generic for Rimadyl). She told me that I would see the difference in a day or so. Shelby took one-half of a tablet in the morning and the other half in the evening. By the second day, she was trotting and running. After a week, she went to just one-half a tablet a day, until her limp got worse and she had stopped trotting and running. I began to give her a half a tablet in the morning and in the evening, and that got her back to trotting and running again. When I mentioned my action to her vet, her vet said that she might have some pain, so she prescribed Tramadol to be used for the pain when necessary.

In the autumn of 2022, Shelby had an extreme case of diarrhea. I tried what we had used before—Pepto Bismal and Imodium AD—but nothing would abate it. I concluded that she had an intestinal virus. After seeing her vet, she prescribed Metronidazole (generic for Flagyl) every twelve hours for ten days. It took only a few days for the diarrhea to stop. After that, anytime Shelby has diarrhea, one to three doses accomplishes the task of bringing the diarrhea to a halt.

The latest drug was introduced into Shelby's diet in the spring of 2023. After noticing that she was restless during the night, often licked the bolsters on her bed or rugs, always wanted to eat grass when outside, and doing some online research, I concluded that she had acid reflux. I began to give her a daily twenty-milligram Omeprazole capsule. After a few days, the acid reflux stopped, she stopped licking her bed and rugs and trying to eat grass, and she began to sleep through the night. That over-the-counter drug is now a part of her daily medicine. Her vet told me that Omeprazole was good for dogs, who had acid reflux.

After having noticed that Shelby's poop was usually very soft, I did some online research and found Bernie's Perfect Poop, a digestion support supplement, which helped harden Shelby's poop and aide her digestion. A few tablespoons a day gives her prebiotics, probiotics, and enzymes. It has also helped in stopping her occasional diarrhea.

Dog modern medicine has enabled Shelby to live a long, happy, and healthy life.

Reflection Questions

1. What medicine(s) does (do) your pet take? Identify what each accomplishes?

2. How does (do) your pet's medicine(s) help your pet live a long, happy, and healthy life? Explain.

11

Diet (Food)

AFTER TRIAL AND ERROR concerning Shelbydog's diet, her veterinarian helped me sort out what food was best for her. Her vet helped me determine that she needed no foods with fat in them, even though she loved cheese, cooked chicken skin, and ground beef. Instead of just measuring food, her vet taught me to count calories.

So, we settled on a diet of basic kibble, lamb and rice; she gets a half of a cup of kibble three times a day. In addition to that, three times a day—morning, noon, and evening—she gets one strip of chicken jerky, a few bites of turkey and venison canned dog food into which are placed her medicines, a large and a small flavored milk bone, and, once a day, a dental bone. This diet helps to maintain her weight and keeps her from throwing up her food after eating it. Unlike most dogs, Shelby is not able to digest all her food at one time.

Shelbydog is very particular about her food; there is some food she does not like, and she will not eat it. Her favorite cooked food is chicken. She gets a few bites of cooked chicken breast on her regular meals; it serves as a motivator for her to clean her bowl.

After she eats her dinner, she often lies by my chair, while I eat my dinner. She does that in the hope that she will get a bite from my plate. If it is something she can have, I give her a bite—a small taste—of whatever I am having for dinner. She can have a bite of chicken, salmon, or beef. She cannot have pasta, bacon, or meat loaf; when I'm eating something she cannot have, I give her a bite broken off of a Milk Bone. I've told her, "I hope you taste what I taste, when I share a morsel of food from my plate with you at dinnertime."

Many people are not aware that the word *companion* means *sharing bread*. Companion is composed from the Latin *com,* meaning *with,* and the French *pain,* meaning *bread.* Thus, etymologically, a companion is one with whom one shares bread. In one way or another, most people share food and more with their pets.

Reflection Questions

1. What is in your pet's diet?

2. How many times a day do you feed your pet? Why?

3. How is your pet your companion?

12

Acid Reflux

S HELBY'S ACID REFLUX GOES back to Thanksgiving Day, November 24, 2022. Before that day I had gone online and read several articles about acid reflux in dogs. Shelby displayed some of the symptoms of the disease, but I was not sure she had it. However, Thanksgiving night, after we had gone to bed, she spent a lot of time smacking her lips, while sitting in her bed. She was also licking the bolsters on her bed, like she had something on her tongue that she was trying to get off. Three or four times before midnight that evening I got up and prepared two antacid tablets in soft dog food and gave them to her. They enabled her to go back to sleep for about an hour, until the acid reflux awakened her again, and I repeated the process.

In addition to the lip smacking and the restlessness, I noticed that on walks Shelby was attempting to eat a lot of grass. While I wasn't 100 percent sure that she had acid reflux, I knew that antacid tablets stopped whatever it was that was bothering her during the night. She didn't have acid reflux every night; it was an occasional thing. When I noticed that she had been licking her bed, I would get up and prepare two antacid tablets for her. Sometimes, that was all it took for the rest of the night; other times I had to repeat the process two or three times.

By early 2023, the acid reflux symptoms were manifesting themselves more frequently during the night, as they do in older dogs. Thus, in the spring of 2023, I went online and re-read several articles about acid reflux in dogs. Similar to humans, a dog's stomach produces acid necessary for food digestion. Also similar to humans, the acid often goes to the base of the esophagus, where it causes heart burn. I noticed that Shelby had begun to display the symptoms of acid reflux more frequently. She was getting up during the night to go get a drink of water, which diluted the acid. She was licking the bolsters on her bed more in her attempt to get the acid off her tongue. And when she was outside, she often tried to eat grass. By late March, the acid reflux nights had become more frequent, but the antacid tablets seemed to be helping Shelbydog. After taking a couple of them, she usually went back to sleep for a few hours, but they were not addressing the problem; they were only addressing the symptoms. Once or twice during the night was OK with me, but then it became three and sometimes four times during the night. I knew that something else had to be done.

At first I tried Nexium caplets, but that gave her diarrhea. So, I switched to Omeprazole delayed release capsules. It took four days for the morning, daily medicine to take effect, but, when it did, she began to sleep throughout the night. And the Omeprazole did not give her diarrhea. When I mentioned this to her vet, she concurred that Omeprazole was a good choice to stop the production of acid in her stomach. Omeprazole turns off the acid-secreting ducts in her stomach.

Once the Omeprazole took effect, both Shelbydog and I began to get an all-night sleep again. Thus, by mid-April 2023, Shelby's sitting in bed, lip smacking, licking her bed, and eating grass had stopped. Now, every morning she gets an Omeprazole capsule with the rest of her daily medicine.

Reflection Questions

1. If you have an older pet, does he or she display any symptoms of acid reflux?

2. Why is it important to diagnose acid reflux in pets?

13

Diarrhea

As long as I have known her, Shelby has always had occasional diarrhea, and if it weren't liquid poop, it was very soft poop. At first, with her vet's help, we determined that her diarrhea was caused by her diet. Once we eliminated some fatty food, her diarrhea was reduced to just once every few weeks. In 2021, her vet gave her a prescription drug to stop it. I only used the prescription drug when Pepto Bismal or Immodium AD would not arrest it. Often, it was caused by Shelby finding something along a sidewalk or trail or in a yard and eating it. Because she liked to submerge herself in cold, flowing, mountain streams and drink from the stream, her diarrhea was also caused by the water she drank.

After having diarrhea, Shelby would not eat her food. The only way I could get her to take her medicine, which was usually given to her in her food bowl, was to wrap it in soft dog food, place it in a small dish, and bring it to her, holding it near her mouth until she licked it out of the small bowl.

Most of the time, diarrhea struck during the night. Shelby would get up and paw my bed until she awakened me. Then, she would go to the rug, sit on it, and face the door. Usually, she would begin to breath very hard, like she was hot. I'd ask, "Do you need to go outside?" and she would stand up with tail wagging and walk to the door leading into the garage and, from there, to the back yard. The onset of diarrhea followed a pattern: very soft poop, liquid poop, more liquid poop.

In early November 2022, she got a case of severe diarrhea, which nothing would stop; one night she got me up two times, and the next night she got me up four times, and a few nights later she got me up five times.

After making an appointment with her vet, we went to see the vet, who thought she had an intestinal virus, which she most likely got from the leaves in which she likes to play. The vet prescribed Metronidazole (generic for Flagyl), which stopped the diarrhea after two to three doses. Because Shelby could smell the medicine wrapped in soft dog food, I enlisted the help of my neighbor, who gave it to her wrapped in peanut butter. After that, I discovered that cream cheese masks the smell of the medicine. I tried pill pouches, but Shelby didn't like the taste of them either; after taking one with the pill inside, she would regurgitate it. The first course of treatment lasted for ten days, during which the diarrhea stopped. After that was completed, her vet recommended a week's worth of Purina FortiFlora, a canine probiotic supplement. When finishing the week's treatment and noticing that it hardened her poop, I continued to give it to her twice a week until I discovered Bernie's Perfect Poop, a digestion support supplement given three times a day; it really reduced the softness of Shelby's poop. And it had an added benefit: Shelby liked to take it sprinkled over her food.

The supplement reduces gas, stool odor, and bad breath; it improves stool quality and firmness, and it enhances Shelby's healthy immune system and overall health. Shelby's diarrhea has been abated, unless she finds something to eat along the sidewalk, when we take a walk, or she drinks water from a stream or reservoir.

After doing some research and talking to Shelby's veterinarian, I discovered that diarrhea in dogs can be caused by anxiety, caused, for example, by the visit of a friend, the preparation to take a trip, or a visit to the vet. After her vet recommended a calming pro-biotic, I began to give her some before anything that might cause her to be anxious. And it worked. It caused her to relax, and that is exactly what I wanted her to do.

Because Shelby does not tolerate humidity very well, I think the combination of summer heat and high humidity (feels-like temperature) can cause diarrhea. When she gets very hot during a walk or even just being outside and the humidity is high, some diarrhea may occur.

While occasional diarrhea continues in Shelby, I have learned to recognize what causes it. I also have the tools—Metronidazole, Bernie's Perfect Poop, and probiotics—to counter it. One to three doses of Metronidazole arrests it; Bernie's Perfect Poop helps to keep it at bay, and probiotics aid Shelby's digestion to help keep it under control. Keeping Shelby's diarrhea under control has been a hit and miss process, lasting four years, but, after finding the right combination of medicine and other aides, it is easier to manage.

Reflection Questions

1. What are the signs that your pet has diarrhea, or needs to go outside during the night?

2. What causes diarrhea in your pet?

3. What stops diarrhea in your pet?

14

Dressing Up

As long as I have known her, Shelbydog loves to dress up. In other words, she likes to wear things. The first time I discovered this, she was wearing her blanket draped over her back after she got out of bed and was walking through the house.

This helped me understand why she was so cooperative in the morning when I put on her harness—over her head, left front foot, right front foot. After her left front foot limp got worse, we began by slipping the left foot leg strap on first, the head piece, then the right leg.

When it snows, she likes to wear her snow booties. I put one on each foot, and she lifts her legs high in the air as she walks, runs, and plays in the snow. When the snow is wet, the booties keep ice balls from forming in between her toes.

After putting on her harness, Shelby stretches her nose toward me so that I can slip on her bandana. She is known by name in my neighborhood and easily recognized by the bandana she wears every day. Over the course of the years, I have bought her several pink, yellow, and green bandanas, and a variety of people have given her red and blue bandanas in various shades of red and blue. She wears the same bandana, tied together at the opposite corners to form a V shape hanging from her neck, all week long. In 2023, Jenson, a boy down the street, gave her a red bandana, which he loves to see her wear.

After her left foot limp got worse, I found a double shoulder brace for her to wear. I knew that it would not be a problem getting her to wear it, because she likes to put on things. So, after it arrived, I read the directions and figured out how to put it on her. At first, she found it a bit restraining, which is what the brace was supposed to do. After the third time wearing it, she began to let it help her, and it made all the difference. She learned that it helped her trot and run, when she wanted to trot or run. It helped her both climb up and down steps. And, of course, she was proud to display it to her friends, who always asked what it was and why she was wearing it.

Now, for daily walks, first I put on her harness. Then, I put on her double shoulder brace. Once that is in place, I put on her bandana, open the door, and off we go. Shelby not only loves to dress up—wear things—but she also loves to show her friends, my neighbors, what she has on.

When she came to live with me, she had a sweater to wear when it got very cold in the winter. However, the sweater did not cover all her back to her tail. So, using the sweater as a pattern, I made her a coat to wear in the cold winter wind. The outer layer is made from an upholstery fabric with dogs imprinted on it; the inner layer is felt. The head covering looks like a bonnet. One strap goes around her neck, and another strap goes under her belly. That way, she can pee and poop without getting anything on her coat. Because she does not like to feel raindrops, if she has to go outside when it is lightly sprinkling rain, I put her coat on her. The bonnet keeps the rain off of her head, and the rest of the coat keeps the rain off of her back. Shelbydog loves to wear things.

Reflection Questions

1. Does your pet like to dress up (wear things)? Explain.

2. What does your pet wear? Make a list. When does your pet wear each item? Why does your pet wear each item?

15

Bath

G ETTING A BATH USED to spark a crisis for Shelbydog. While she likes getting in a cold, flowing stream or in a foot-deep pool, she did not like getting a bath. In her puppy days, she was sprayed with a hose; it was her first owner's attempt to discipline her. All it did was damage her psychologically. However, over the course of the past four years, she has learned that a bath can be an enjoyable experience.

I begin talking about a bath four or five days before it is going to take place. On the day of the bath, I spread extra rugs on the bathroom floor in front of the walk-in shower. Then, I place her dog-wash shampoo in a handy place and get her two towels and put them close by. I call her to come to the bathroom to get her bath; in the past she would not come—I would have to get her and lead her into the bathroom—but now she comes, when I call.

She comes into the bathroom and sits in front of the shower. I close the bathroom door. Then, I pick her up using her harness and put her front feet intothe shower, then pick up her rear end and push her into the shower. After removing her harness, I take the detachable shower nozzle, and, without spraying—merely moving it over her—wet her from head to tail. She loves the cold water wetting her fur. Then, I spread dog wash shampoo all over her and rub it into her fur. After putting more shampoo in my hands, I go over each leg separately and her tail until she is covered from nose to tail in suds. Then, taking the shower nozzle again and moving it over her, I rinse off the suds beginning with her head, back, then her belly, and finally all four legs and tail. Once the water is running clear, I know all the soap

32

has been removed. After shutting off the water, I tell her to stand still for a few minutes and drip. Then, I take a towel and spread it over her, rubbing it over he back and legs to dry her a little.

I tell her to step out of the shower, and she gets out and stands on the extra rug. I take another towel and dry her from nose to tail, drying each leg separately, her tail separately, and in between her toes on each foot. Once that is accomplished, she is ready to run out of the bathroom and through the house, when I open the bathroom door. I follow her to the front porch, where I roll her on her back and dry under her shoulders and belly and tail. Once I'm sure I've dried all I can, I leave her in the sun, which completes the drying process.

Because she was sprayed with a hose at one time in her life, that action made giving her a bath a major task. Over the years I have coached her and shown her that a bath will not hurt her. On the contrary, it makes her feel good and happy. After I talk about it for several days, she is ready to get it. Several times after eating her breakfast she has gone to the bathroom and sat in front of the shower without me calling her. On one occasion, she has stepped into the shower and waited for me to begin the bath process. By changing her experience of getting a bath, I have changed her attitude about it. Gradually, she has been overcoming a past negative experience and letting me transform getting a bath into a positive experience.

Reflection Questions

1. Does your pet like to get a bath? Explain.

2. Is a bath a positive or negative experience for your pet? Explain.

3. Is a bath for your pet a positive or negative experience for you? Explain.

16

Humidity and Heat

T HERE IS NO DOUBT that Shelbydog prefers late autumn, winter, and early spring. While she loves cool weather, she hates the humidity and heat of summer. In fact, she will go for a walk when it is hot, but will not when the humidity is high. She doesn't want to be outside in the humidity. As the Missouri humidity abates in the fall, she is ready and willing to take long walks and smell bushes, trees, and grass. It is easy to tell that the fading humidity makes her feel better, because she is ready to walk three times a day and to travel farther. Also, she breaks into trots and runs at times.

In the summer, we change our walking habits. We try to take our long walk early in the morning before it gets too humid and hot. If the humidity is high, we only go for a one-block walk after lunch or we go to the back yard. After dinner, we walk only two blocks—and sometimes only one—when it is above 80-degrees or the humidity is 60 percent or higher.

The simple fact is that Shelbydog cannot handle the humidity. It causes her to slow down on walks; the closer we get to home, the slower she gets in the humidity and heat. Furthermore, as her age increases, her tolerance for humidity and heat decreases. As the humidity and heat increase, the distance we walk decreases. After even a short walk in the humidity and heat, Shelby comes home hot and tired. The first thing she does once she gets into the house is to lie spread-eagle on the cool tile floor. On humid and hot days, Shelby prefers to stay indoors in the air conditioning rather than being outside for a walk or with me when I am doing something in the back yard. At night, I run a window air conditioner in our bedroom; it not only reduces more of the humidity that gets into the house, but it also keeps it very cool for both of us to sleep well. Shelby is a winter dog; she likes the cold weather without humidity.

The high humidity affects her left leg that has joint inflammation. When the humidity and heat increase, she limps more. As a result, we have to decrease how far we walk on humid and hot days. A double daily dose of Carprofen, her anti-inflamatory drug, helps the discomfort she feels in her left shoulder on humid and hot days.

To escape the heat and humidity, over the past years we have spent a month of summer in Colorado, where the humidity is low—or non-existent—and the daytime temperature seldom reaches 80 degrees. Shelby loves the cold mountain mornings and the cool mountain evenings. While the mid-day temperature may be warmer, the lack of humidity enables her to walk, trot, and run. While she gets hot, a little water cools her.

I have often referred to her brindle coat as a solar panel. She absorbs heat like a solar panel absorbs sunshine. Even though she sheds some of her fine under fur in the spring and early summer, she still wears a fur coat the rest of the year. Her color—brindle with red highlights—attracts sunlight, which makes her hot. I know she is hot when I see her mouth open and her tongue hanging out. The degree of her hotness is illustrated by how far her tongue hangs out of her mouth!

Thus, when in our own environment, we cope with the humidity and the heat by taking short walks and staying in the air conditioned house.

Reflection Questions

1. How does humidity affect your pet?

2. How does humidity affect you?

3. How does heat affect your pet?

4. How does heat affect you?

5. Is there any connection between the way humidity and heat affect your pet and the way humidity and heat affect you? Explain.

17

Routines

S HELBY LOVES ROUTINE; SHE is a dog of routines. After she arises in the morning, she walks to the front porch to see what is going on outside the glass door. I call her to come and get ready for her walk, and she comes and sits on one of her favorite rugs. I put on her harness, double-shoulder brace, and bandana. I say, "You're ready for your walk." She goes back to the front porch, where she waits for me to gather her water bottle, poop bags, and leash, and for me to put on my hat or my jacket or coat. I pick up a key and meet her at the front door, where I attach her leash to her harness ring. I open the door and tell her, "Slowly and gently down the steps." Once she reaches the last step, I turn around and lock the door. Then I say, "Let's go," and we begin.

Our morning walk is always the same route. I read an online article about changing the dog's usual walking routine. I tried changing hers, but Shelby plants all four feet and will not go in a different direction! She doesn't want anything different; she wants to walk the same sidewalk in the morning, noon, and evening. She wants to cross the streets at specific places; it gives her the security of knowing the way.

So, we walk one block east, then one block south, then four blocks west, one block north, and four blocks east back home. Shelby may want to cross the sidewalk a few times because of something she smells or someone she sees and knows. Along the walk, she stops to poop and waits for me to retrieve a green plastic bag from my pocket and pick up her poop. We stop in the same place for me to give her a drink of water. We take the same route every morning.

We have a similar routine for our after-lunch walk. After gathering the poop bag, water bottle, leash, key, and my (coat and) hat, we proceed to cross the street and, after one block, walk north three blocks. On hot days, Shelby stops under shade trees in a few spots to roll and wiggle. Our destination is a garden in a park with both a stone bench and a picnic table. Shelby hops on either the bench or the table to rest and get a drink. Once that is accomplished, we head north behind a large church with a Montessori school. Shelby likes the teacher to open the playground gate and let the students pet her and talk to her. After that we move toward a large oak tree, where we stop to get another drink of water. Then, we head west for a block or two (depending on hot the day is), then south two blocks, then east two blocks to home.

Our routine evening walk begins with us crossing the street to walk west under trees and out of the sun. After two blocks west, we usually turn north and walk one block, then two blocks east, then two blocks south, then one block west and home.

Shelby has a routine when she goes to the back yard. She goes to a grassy area, where she pees, then she investigates the whole yard traveling on the walkways south, east, north, and west to the back door, where she indicates that she is ready to go inside.

Inside the house, she has routines. When someone appears at the front door, she picks up one of her toys and prepares to share it with a visitor. When she crosses by her toy box, she will often stop and look at what is inside. Sometimes she chooses an item and takes it with her to the front porch, her favorite room in the house. Other times, she takes nothing out of her toy box.

At morning feeding after our morning walk, she comes to the kitchen door and lies on the tile floor, watching me as I prepare her breakfast. If she doesn't move, I know she wants to eat lying with her paws on either side of her white porcelain bowl. If she moves to the rug in the kitchen, I know she wants to eat her breakfast on the rug upon which rests her water bowl in the kitchen.

The same routine occurs during lunch. When she hears me turn on the TV to watch the noonday news, she comes to the kitchen door. Likewise, in the evening, when she hears the TV, she comes to get her dinner.

She has a routine for going to bed in the winter, and she has a routine for falling asleep on the front porch in the summer, having me awaken her and tell her, "It's time to go to bed," after which she gets up and walks to her bed in the bedroom.

Once she lies upon her bed, I pet her, pray with her, and cover her with her blanket from nose to tail. She falls asleep quickly, while I prepare to get into my bed.

In the morning, her routine, after she awakens, is to lie in her bed for a while, then arise, walk through the house to see where I am, and go to the front porch to see what is going on outside. She may decide to go to the living room rug, where she lies on her back and wiggles and rolls. After I call her to come get ready for her walk, she comes and sits on her favorite rug, I get her ready, and off we go to begin the routine of a new day.

With Shelby's limp getting worse and less pounding of limbs on the sidewalk was necessary, we had to adjust our routine walks. That was not easy to do! We reduced all walks to one square block. Shelby usually wanted to continue the former route. It took a lot of coaching over two weeks for me to get her to cut short the walk or alter the route.

Reflection Questions

1. What are your pet's routines? Make a list.

2. For each routine ask: What security does this routine give my pet? Note your answer after the routine?

3. As you look over the list of your pet's routines and the security each gives your pet, what conclusion can you reach?

18

Fan Club (Friends)

T HROUGHOUT THE NEIGHBORHOOD, SHELBY has a fan club. Her brindle fur with red highlights attracts people to her. Her usually labeled "sweet disposition" invites neighbors to pet her, to scratch behind her ears, and to give her bellyrubs when she lies on her back at their feet with her feet in the air and her belly exposed. Because she is a solitary dog, she is very careful in her choice of friends. While some people will attempt to befriend her, she will not always reciprocate!

These are people who like to interact with her and to whom she will respond: Michelle will stop her vehicle in the street and get out of it to pet Shelbydog. Adrianne and her mother, fellow walkers, will always stop to pet and talk to Shelbydog. Bob, an early morning walker, will cross the street, talk to Shelby, and pet her. Ray, another walker, often stops as we cross paths with him on the streets in our neighborhood and talk to Shelby.

One of Shelby's favorite friends is Matthew. She gets very excited when I drive to the airport with her in the back seat, and Matthew gets into the Jeep. She sits in the back seat with her head placed between the front seats in order to see him. He is one of the few people she will let walk her without me being present. While visiting us, she will lie at his feet and beg for attention and bellyrubs. She will beg food from him, while we are eating. And she will sit near the guest bedroom door awaiting his emergence in the morning. After he spends a few days with us, she is sad when we take him back to the airport. After we get home, she doesn't want to walk, eat, or play.

Likewise, when we are in Colorado, he comes to visit for a day or two. He talks to her and pets her. And she likes to go on hikes with him. Just recently she demonstrated how much she likes him by climbing onto his bed and spending part of the night lying beside him.

Most of our mail carriers are Shelby's friends. The current mailwoman waits for me to open the door and for Shelby to emerge with her duckie. After Misty takes duckie, she gives him back to Shelby, who sits on the step so Misty can pet her. When we have a substitute carrier that we know, the same process takes place. Over the years I have trained mail carriers how to interact with Shelby. Sometimes we get a carrier we do not know; he or she is always in a hurry. I remember one such occasion when I opened the door to receive the mail—Shelby had indicated that the carrier was approaching by barking—and I closed the door and turned around to find Shelby sitting behind me with duckie in her mouth and looking heartbroken because she did not get to share her duckie with the carrier. I petted her, hugged her, and gave her a bellyrub because she was so sad. After a few minutes of one-on-one attention, she felt better.

Another of her mail-carrier friends is Matt. Usually, he substitutes once a week. She likes to bring her duckie to him, because he knows what to do. He always talks to her and pets her head.

Another special friend is Marsha. When Marsha appears in her car in the driveway, Shelby takes either duckie or deerie out to greet her, as she emerges from her car. Then, she leads her up the steps and into the house. Throughout Marsha's visit, Shelby sits near her, lies at her feet, or solicits a bellyrub from her.

Another of Shelby's friends is Kris. She likes to see him, when he stops by to visit. Usually, she runs to greet him with one of her toys in her mouth. After he comes in and sits, she makes it a point to sit on the floor by his chair and solicit bellyrubs from him. She likes going to his house, too. He has a dog named Bo, and Shelby and Bo like to play both outside and inside his house. Most of the time they chase each other through the rooms.

Shelby has friends in Fertile, Missouri, in the house where we live when we are in my hometown. She likes to see Sam, the cook, with whom she spends a lot of time in the kitchen. Sam talks to her, and Shelby loves to be talked to; Sam often watches her if I have to be away. Shelby also likes Sam's husband, Richard. He talks to her, pets her, and gives her bellyrubs. Shelby will go up the stairs to visit Kathy in her office. Kathy, too, talks to her. Both Sam and Kathy will take her on walks. Shelby lets Sam and Kathy walk her.

Another of her friends in Fertile is Neva. Not only will Shelby walk with Neva, but she will play with Neva, who finds duckie and brings duckie to her. Neva will spend a lot of time petting and bellyrubbing Shelby. Natalie is another of Shelby's friends; Natalie talks to her and pets her. When I take her for walks in Fertile, she never wants to go very far, because she wants to get back inside and sit by the door and wait for her friends to arrive. If one or more of her friends accompany her on a trail near their property, she will walk the trail with them. In the morning, she will wait for her friends to arrive before eating her breakfast.

Another of Shelby's friends is Mike. She gets very excited when I tell her he is coming to visit. When she sees his car in the driveway, she finds duckie and runs out to greet him. While he visits, she spends a lot of time lying at his feet and soliciting bellyrubs from him. Because he accompanies us on some trips, Shelby likes it when he takes care of her, taking her on walks, and talking to her. She also likes it when he gives her treats. She has visited him in his home and spent part of a day with him.

On our morning walks through the neighborhood, we often encounter a lady, who crosses our path and gives Shelby a small treat from her pocket. After this occurred the first time, Shelby remembers every subsequent time we see the lady walking. She moves toward the woman and sits in front of her awaiting a small, bite-size treat.

Some of the latest members of Shelby's fan club include a family: Billy, Melissa, Jasper, and Jenson. After reading her book, *The Shelbydog Chronicles*, they celebrated her eleventh birthday with a balloon, an acrostic composed from her name (see Chapter 27), a cloth neck wrap, and a cloth bone. They spent time with her, talking to her, petting her, and giving her a bellyrub. Melissa tells Shelby how much she loves her. And Jenson gives her bellyrub after bellyrub. Billy, whom we see often on the front porch reading on the weekends, talks to her a lot and pets her, scratching behind her ears. Their home is one of her favorite places to stop on a walk. She knows exactly where they live. Either they see us through a window or I ring the doorbell and they emerge through the front door with their little dog, Lucy, and talk to Shelby and pet her. Lucy and Shelby exchange nose sniffs. Shelby especially likes Jenson, whom she licks over and over again!

Shelby likes our neighbor Sheryl, who talks to her and pets her. While Shelby will not go for a walk with Sheryl, she likes to see Sheryl when she visits or when she is working in her yard. Sheryl's husband, Chris, is also one of Shelby's friends. If she sees him outside or she sees him getting out of his truck, she heads toward him. He talks to her and pets her.

She likes Adrianne, who comes once a month to clean the house. Throughout the time she is present, Adrianne talks to her and pets her. While Adrianne is cleaning, Shelby will leave her front porch room, find her, and spend time watching her clean. On one occasion, Maison, our handyman, was present when Adrianne was cleaning. Shelby likes Maison, who talks to her and pets her. That day, Shelby couldn't decide with which friend she would spend more time.

Shelby used to have a dog friend named Conan, but he got too big for her to play with him. She also has a friend, named Auge, who lives behind a fence. He and Shelby often rub noses through the fence, when we pass by on the sidewalk on our morning walk.

In the spring of 2023, Shelby became a member of the six-year-old Montessori class down the street. When taking our post-lunch walk, we had often passed the playground upon which the Roses were playing. One day the teacher asked me if it were OK for the students to pet Shelby. I said yes, and she opened the gate; the students came out and petted and petted Shelby. As they talked to her and petted her, Shelby solicited bellyrubs from them. The teacher used the occasion to teach them about dogs. Thereafter, the students would watch for us to come by daily. When they spotted us coming around the corner of the building, they began to shout, "Shelby, Shelby." She would begin to wag her tail and head toward them. After school was dismissed for the summer, Shelby continued to look for her class, when we passed by the playground on our daily walk.

We used to see more of Shelby's friend Barbara, but we see less of her now that we do not walk by her house as often as we used to. Shelby used to pull me toward Barbara's house, where we would approach a door, I'd ring the bell, and Shelby would put her ear to the door to hear if Barbara was coming to open it. If she were home, she'd open the door and Shelby would walk in. Barbara would give her a bowl of water and/or a treat; we'd visit for a few minutes and, then, leave. If Barbara were not home, Shelby would lead me to the other door, where I'd ring the bell and Shelby would put her ear to the door to hear if Barbara were coming. I couldn't get Shelby to understand that if Barbara was not at the back door, she was also not at the front door, or vice-versa!

The owner of the apartment, in which we stay in Colorado, is another one of Shelby's friends. Janet, who owns her own dog—Girlfriend—always greets and talks to Shelby and pets her. Because Janet has a workshop under the apartment, Shelby wants to go see what she is doing, when she hears the garage doors open under the apartment.

Bill and Kathy are other Colorado friends of Shelby. While she likes visiting them and exploring their fenced-in back yard, she likes following Bill wherever he goes. Both Bill and Kathy talk to her, pet her, and acknowledge her presence. She likes to lie in the middle of their dining room/living room floor on her back and solicit bellyrubs from both of them. Shelby is fascinated by the sounds around their home, such as the sprinkler system, coyotes, and coal train whistles. After we leave there, Shelby is sad because she misses following Bill and exploring his backyard.

The Kosslers—John, Amy, Ethan, and Jacob—are more of Shelby's Colorado friends. She likes to hike with them, and even lets Ethan and Jacob hold on to her leash. Ethan has to keep his distance, as he is allergic to dogs. But John talks to her and pets her, Amy talks to her and pets her, and Jacob talks to her and pets her. Ethan talks to her and enjoys being as close to her as he can get. While she only sees the Kosslers once a year, she remembers them from year to year.

There are other neighbors who, if they are outside or working in their yards, will call Shelby by name and come over and pet her, or they will call her to come to them and they will pet her. They are attracted to her by her color and friendly disposition. In other words, Shelby is the queen of the neighborhood, and neighbors treat her as such. That is why I refer to all of them as members of her fan club.

Reflection Questions

1. Who are the friends of your pet? Make a list.

2. What do your pet's friends say about your pet?

19

Peculiarities

W HEN SHELBYDOG WENT INTO cat mode or lay on her back with all four feet in the air and wiggled or did something else not generic to dogs, her former owner used to say, "How strange!" Shelby's peculiarities are what make her unique.

While it doesn't happen too often, if Shelby is outside with me and someone—like the postal carrier, UPS carrier, or FedEx carrier—walks onto the driveway, she barks at the person, and she raises her hackles. Most people understand raised hackles as a sign that they are about to be attacked. That is not the case with Shelby. As I tell anyone walking down the driveway, "She will not hurt you. I do not know how to make her not raise her hackles."

Another of Shelby's peculiarities is her like of sawdust. When she finds sawdust, it gives her great pleasure to roll in it. On one occasion on a walk we found sawdust near an electric pole; a new pole had been inserted into the ground near the old one, which had been cut off at the top with a chainsaw. Until Shelby stopped rolling in the sawdust, I had no idea that the sawdust had engine oil or chainsaw oil mixed in with it. As we continued our walk, Shelby smelled like motor oil, so she had to have a bath after we got home. She also likes to roll around and wiggle in mulch. When a load of mulch is delivered to my house and dumped on the driveway, it is common to see Shelby on her back rolling from side to side and wiggling in it!

Shelby likes to catch and eat flies and bees. In the spring, I often find her in the back yard beneath a red bud tree jumping up toward its branches attempting to catch the bees visiting its blossoms. Also, she looks for bees in the flower gardens.

On walks, when I stop for a few minutes to visit with a fellow walker, Shelby lies and gets bored waiting for me to continue our walk. So, she looks for grass leaves to eat. Repeatedly, during my conversation with another walker, I have to tell her not to eat grass. Sometimes, she will stand and point in the direction we were headed in an effort to get me to continue our walk.

At home, especially for breakfast but for other meals too, Shelby likes to eat while she is spread-eagle on the floor. I put her bowl of food between her front paws, and she dips her head into her bowl to eat her food. She tells me where she wants to eat her meals. If she sits or lies in the doorway between the dining room and the kitchen, it means she wants to eat while lying on the floor. If she comes to the kitchen and sits on the rug in front of the sink, it means she wants to eat her meal while standing near the rug where her water bowl is located.

She has a keen awareness of her size and where she can fit or pass. If I have my feet resting on an ottoman, she knows that she can pass under them. In the backyard garden, she knows what plants she can walk under and which ones she needs to walk around. In the house, she knows what furniture she can walk between and not get stuck. There are places in which she finds that the only way she can move forward is that she has to move backward!

Shelby is very nosey and loves to explore garages. In mine, she explores boxes and recycling bins. On walks, when she sees a neighbor's garage door open, she wants to go and explore it. She also loves the cars and trucks parked in garages. An open car door or truck door is an invitation to her to jump in and go for a ride. I used to say to her, "Do you want to go for a ride?" and she would respond by running through the house to the back door, which opened into the garage. After a while, she began to associate the jingle of my car keys with going for a ride. Now, all I have to do is jingle the car keys, and she comes running through the house with her tail curled high and ready to jump into the backseat of the car. As she watches me get ready for a trip, I tell her, "You can go," and she gets all excited; she runs through the house with her tail curled toward her head and held high in the air.

While she listens to me, Shelby often expresses herself by raising her eyebrows and raising, lowering, twitching, and drawing her ears closer to her head. She has the ability to pull her left ear close to her head—which indicates attentive listening—while leaving the right ear in the pointed, listening position. She is very cute when she is listening attentively!

Because Shelby has sprained her left paw twice—once playing with her dog friend, Conan, and once falling into a hole—when she lies on a rug and curls it up under her, I often take it and straighten it.

She does not like getting hot. If she knows it is hot outside, she will not want to go for a walk. When she gets hot on walks, she pulls toward the shade under a tree, where she will roll around in the grass. On a hike, she likes to get into a stream so that the water flows over her back with only her head elevated above the water. At home when she gets hot, she finds a cool place on the tile floor or near an air conditioning vent—she knows where all of them are in the hous—and lies spread eagle. However, she doesn't like getting wet in the rain. If she feels a single raindrop, she turns around abruptly and heads back home.

She likes to sit in an overstuffed chair by a window in the apartment we rent in Colorado. She places her front paws on an arm of the chair and falls sleep. Or she places her front paws on the back of the chair and leans her head on them to watch whatever is going on outside. At home she likes to lie on a rug in front of a glass door and watch cars—especially if they have lights on—pass by.

Shelby likes to stretch on a rug. When getting ready to go for a walk, a ride, or outside, she puts on her happy face. Then, she puts forth her front paws spread flat on a rug on the tile floor and lowers her head to the floor between them, while keeping her hind quarters in the air and her tail curled and pointing over her back and toward her head! As she stretches, she emits a sigh. She may repeat this three or four times when getting ready to go out.

She likes to rub her back against solid furniture, walls, beds, etc. It is common to see her rubbing her back that way. While she likes to wiggle and roll on the rug in my living room, she doesn't like me catching her doing so. Often, I hear her making noises while enjoying herself rolling from side to side. As soon as she hears my footsteps coming into the room, she stops.

She becomes jealous when friends come to visit me. While we are sitting and engaged in conversation, she will go from one to another and beg to be petted or solicit bellyrubs by lying on her back with all four feet in the air.

I have come to understand that many of Shelby's peculiarities come from her wolf DNA. I see it in her ferocious barking, in her curiosity about everything, in her red wolf highlights, in her lying wherever she is when she is tired, in her playfulness, in her alpha consciousness, in her careful choice of friends, and in her solitariness. I think her wolf genes are manifest in her brindle color; I have a photo of a Central European wolf, which looks exactly like Shelby—same size, same short nose, same pointed ears, same cream-colored belly fur, and same brindle fur with red highlights. Shelby does not have the bushy tale that the Central European wolf displays; it was probably bred out of her ancestors over the years. As a domestic dog, she prefers to be inside the house, but as a wolf she still possesses some fierce-ness—raising her hackles—and she looks for rabbits in bushes. Her barking at passersby and growling are wolf characteristics. Her begging for petting and bellyrubs illustrate that she is a domestic dog. Shelby's attentiveness to sounds is also a wolf characteristic.

After talking to a friend with a degree in psychology, I learned that light on a cloudy day helps many people with seasonal depression. So, because Shelby loves sunshine so much, spending most of her day lying in it, I bought her a light lamp. When the day is cloudy or rainy, I turn on the lamp, and she lies under it, as if it were the sun. When we are in Colorado, she spends less time in the sun than she does at home, because it is more intense at higher elevations.

When she wants something from me, she finds me and lays her head on my knee and looks at me with her big brown eyes. She usually wants a bellyrub. So, I get out of my chair and sit by her on the floor, roll her onto her side, and rub her belly. This goes on until she's had enough, gets up, and walks away.

In the autumn, after some of the leaves have fallen off of the trees, Shelby likes to walk through the thickest piles, and she likes to roll around in them. Also, she likes to pee on them and to poop in them. On a walk, she will want to move from one side of the street to the other, if she spots a pile of leaves.

In the house, she will often appear behind a door frame, peaking at me, usually in my office. She has to see what I am doing. If I see her, I call her, and she comes to me. I pet her head and pat her back for a minute; then, she goes back to the front porch, where she likes to spend her time.

When petting Shelby's head and stopping, she will often put her nose under my hand and lift it up in order to indicate that she wants more head petting or scratching behind her ears. Sometimes she comes and sits beside me and turns so that her back is toward me. That means that she wants her back scratched. At other times, when she is being petted, she raises either her left or right front paw in the air to indicate that she wants more. When she is sitting, the raising of a left or right front paw can mean that she wants to be petted, she wants to play, she wants to awaken me from a nap, she wants to go outside, or she wants to take a walk. While she is is being petted or receiving a bellyrub, she likes to touch my arm, hand, leg, or foot with either her left or right front paw; it is her way of being connected to me.

She likes to be near me. If I am in the living room, she wants to be on the front porch (the room closest), on the floor by my chair, or on the rug in the middle of the floor. If I'm in the dining room, she wants to be on the rug in that room. If I'm in the bedroom, she's in the bedroom lying or sitting on the rug or in or on her bed. If I'm working in my office, she comes in from time to time and either sits on the rug for a while or sits near my office chair. In other words, Shelby likes to spend a lot of time with me.

Because she likes to spend time with me, she also has to deal more intensely with separation anxiety. I used not to be able to leave her alone without coming home to find something done, like pillows pulled off the couch or rugs rolled up. Now, I tell her that I will be gone for a certain length of time and she cannot go along, and when I get home, she has remained in her favorite room: the front porch. Separation anxiety still manifests itself when I am sick and unable to take her for a walk. She will not go for a walk with my neighbors, unless I go along. Recently, when I was sick, I called my neighbor to come and take Shelby for a walk. She would not go more than one-half a block. The neighbor brought her back, saying, "She is a one-man dog." There are a few other friends, however, with whom she will walk without me.

Shelbydog loves steps. She likes both going up them and coming down them. When we visit the university, she likes to run up the long staircases and hop from one step to the next down them. In a place we often stay when visiting my hometown, she likes to run up the steps at one end of the building, run across the second floor, and hop down the steps at the other end of the building. After doing so, she, panting, finds me to tell me how happy she is.

Shelby loves cold weather and snow. While I'm all bundled with long-johns, sweater, coat, double gloves, and double cap, Shelby only needs her coat to walk in the winter snow and ice. While she likes walking in the snow, she also likes following me as I shovel the driveway. She likes to stand or sit right behind me in the path that I have cleared, as I make my way with the snow shovel over the driveway and from side to side, removing snow. After I finish shoveling the driveway, I usually take her for a walk in the snow. She likes to run through snow drifts, but she also likes to walk on cleared sidewalks. When the snow is wet, she has a set of four booties I put on her feet to keep the snow from turning into ice balls between her toes. She likes putting on the booties, but she raises her feet high when she wears them!

If she can see her medicine or smell it in her soft dog food, she will not take it. While soft dog food usually serves the purpose, I've had to be creative with some medicines. A small amount of cream cheese will mask the more fragrant tablets she takes, when I give them to her one at a time. At other times, wrapped in soft dog food and placed in her food bowl with her kibble and chicken jerky pieces mask any smells enough that she consumes them while eating her meal.

My philosophy is that I treat Shelby like a dog when she acts like a dog, being stubborn, refusing to cooperate, not doing what she has been told to do, eating something along the sidewalk, rolling in mud, scratching a rug, etc. When she acts like the smart dog I know she is, she gets praised, petted, and bellyrubbed.

Once Shelby gets focused on watching a cat, watching a person, watching cars with head lights pass, etc., I have to tug her leash and talk to her, as if awakening her to rejoin reality. She gets mesmerized and is so focused that she loses all sense of place or time. Her focused time on something or someone gets longer as she gets older.

When she sleeps, she likes to hang her front paws off the bed or chair with her head resting on her front paws. As she ages, she also wears out faster and needs more sleep. She sleeps in the back seat of the car, when we travel. She spends a lot of her day lying in the sunshine and sleeping either on her belly or on her side at home.

In Shelby's world, cats are supposed to run away from dogs. However, the neighbor's cat was raised with a dog; thus, she is not scared of dogs. At two different times, Vera, the cat, has emerged, walked to Shelby lying on the driveway, and, while purring, licked Shelby's nose. That action has paralyzed Shelby; she does not know what to do, because there is a cat in front of her who is not scared of her and is not running away from her! Now, when Shelby sees Vera, she moves away from her. If Vera continues to walk toward her, Shelby moves farther away. In some instances, I have to take Shelby home, because she keeps pulling me in that direction to escape a confrontation with Vera!

Shelby has many facial expressions. One time on a walk she slipped into a neighbor's yard, where the neighbor was working in a flower garden. As I talked to Shelby and called her to continue our walk, the neighbor said, "She is expressing herself with her face." I said, "I know; she has many facial expressions."

She has a happy facial expression. She appears with her mouth open, teeth showing, eyes wide open, ears resting in a flipped over position, and smiling. Her sad face features her head resting on the floor with her front paws stretched out on either side and her ears resting in a flipped over position. When Shelby does not understand something I'm saying, she points her ears up and displays a quizzical look on her face, while tilting her head from side to side. When receiving a bellyrub, she displays pleasure with her head on her side, ears pointed up, eyes rolling to the back of her head or eyes closed. When she is listening to me, but not ready to act, she moves her ears up and down and her eye lids up and down, while looking straight ahead.

When Shelby does not get to do what she wants, like go for a ride in the Jeep, she often protests. One of her favorite forms of protest is to go through the house and pull all pillows off beds and couches onto the floor. At home, a favorite form of protest is shredding a rug in the basement. While lying on the end of the rug, she extends her front paws to its edge, and, after embedding her toe nails in its pile, she pulls until she gets threads loose.

At home, her favorite place is the front porch, where she lies on a rug and watches cars pass on a major street. When not watching cars, she sleeps on her side on the cool tile floor. She spends a lot of time alone on the front porch. Likewise, when we visit friends, she often searches for a spot in their homes where she can be alone, such as a deck, sunroom, etc.

In the winter, when the front glass door fogs, Shelby will sit and wait for me to come and wipe the fog from the front door so she can see what is taking place in her world. She moves out of the way so that I can spray the glass and wipe away the fog; then, she moves to her usual place on the rug in front of the door. Often, I will sit behind her, pet her, and talk to her, while she gazes at cars and people passing by.

She knows what most of the ringing bells in the house mean. She knows when the smoke alarm goes off because I burned a slice of toast or something spilled on the stove; she does not like the sound of the smoke alarms. Also, she knows that the doorbell means someone is at the front door; she barks, and heads toward the front door.

While she was still sleeping, one morning I placed some pop tarts in the toaster oven. When the bell rang to tell me that they were sufficiently toasted, she arose from her bed and walked into the kitchen, where she stood and stared at me. She didn't know what the toaster oven bell meant! The next day I put the pop tarts in the microwave, and she didn't get out of bed when that bell rang, because she knew it was the microwave!

While Shelby does not like getting hot, she does like joining me in the sauna during the winter. It is not uncommon for us to head to the outdoor sauna on a cold fall or winter afternoon. Shelby likes to sit on the lowest bench in the sauna. I give her a drink of water, and she lies on the bench, which has a rug on it, for a while until I notice that she is getting too hot. I tell her that it is time for her to get out and lie in the cool vestibule. She jumps down and exits to the vestibule, where it is cool. She lies on the rug and plays with a toy or sleeps. When she is awake, she keeps looking at the sauna door, wondering when she can get back in. I let her back in for a few minutes before I am ready to get out and head back to the house.

Shelby's favorite food is her dental bone. The large Milk Bone Brushing Chew is springy. After she gets it from me, firmly wedged between her teeth, she takes it to her favorite rug and places it firmly between her front paws so that one end of it leans to her left. Once she is sure that she has it secured firmly, she leans her head to her left, opens her mouth, and brings her teeth together on the end and bites off a piece to chew. Then, after chewing and swallowing, she repeats the process until all the bone is gone.

If we stop to visit a neighbor on a walk, I go to the door and either knock or ring the door bell. Shelby goes to the door and puts her head and ear close to it so she can hear anyone coming to open it. If she hears someone approaching, she gets happy. If no one is home—if the door is not opened—she puts on her sad face!

Shelby is a very nosey dog. As mentioned above, she loves to explore garages. However, she also likes to investigate sounds she may hear. If she hears someone outside, she barks and wants to go outside and see what is happening. She likes to watch people do whatever they are doing.

Shelby is a very independent dog. In her solitary times, she does whatever she wants. She gets out of bed during the night and goes to get a drink of water before returning to her bed. When we are in the Colorado apartment, she often falls asleep in her chair and comes to her bed later in the evening. Sometimes, if she is warm, she gets out of her bed during the night and sleeps on the floor or on a rug. At home, she chooses where she wants to nap during the day, where she wants to play, and on walks upon what side of the street she wants to explore.

Shelby knows how to back out of a collar around her neck, if she is tied somewhere. She gets the line to which she is tied very taught and begins to back away. With her head lowered, her collar slips over her head and off onto the ground. Likewise, if she gets snagged on something when she is wearing her harness, she knows how to step out of it and let it slip over her head.

Shelby's peculiarities reveal her personality and make her who she is: a Shelbydog!

Reflection Questions

1. What are you pet's peculiarities? Make a list.

2. What do your pet's peculiarities tell you about your pet?

20

Spirituality

S HELBY POSSESSES A UNIQUE spirit that identifies her as Shelbydog.
Instead of referring to the philosophical designation of soul, I prefer to
use the word *spirit*. Shelby is endowed with spirit, a life principle, a spiritual
life principle. If all that exists does so in God, then she will never go out of
existence, even when she dies. Her short life—in terms of human years—is
designed to accompany me on my journey just as I accompany her on her
journey, as long as she lives. Shelby has been entrusted to me by God—she
is a servant of God—so that I can care for her. God never destroys what
he has created; once being (spirit) becomes incarnate, it never goes out of
existence. It is transformed into another mode of existence. God preserves
all uniqueness because it reveals to him another one of the infinite aspects
of who he is.

Various people around the world believe that spiritual forces are inherent in animals, people, and other natural phenomena. Animals possess
guardian spirits; they are spiritual beings participating in divine Spirit.
Therefore, they are to be treated with respect. They, like everything else in
the world, share a life force, Spirit. The Supreme Being (God, Spirit) is the
personification of the life force which flows through and animates both humans and animals. Thus, both humans and animals share Spirit, the breath
of life. This helps us understand the connection felt between a person and a
dog. Often without being aware both experience a unity, a oneness of being
(spirit)—often called love—which not even death can sever or destroy.

I often refer to Shelby as one of God's servants, just like I am one of
God's servants. Both of us have been created by God and have had the

breath of life (spirit) breathed (inspirited) into us. Every breath we take together is a participation in the divine Spirit, in God's own life. Since life is not ended but changed at death, both of us will pass over to a new spiritual existence that cannot be seen. The spiritual bond we share now will continue past death into eternity.

From time to time, Shelby spends quality time with me. She finds me and we look deeply into each other's spirit. Just as I breathe her spirit, she breathes mine. Just as she lets me touch her deeply, I reciprocate. We can hear each other's spirit. During those spiritual exchanges, both of us become more secure in being ourselves, in being who we truly are. We are companions, literally sharing bread with each other, metaphorically sharing spirit with each other.

Shelby is a very free spirit; when we share spirit with each other, we also understand each other better. Her veterinarian shares her spirit with Shelbydog, too. Thus, God works healing in Shelby over and over again through her veterinarian's wisdom and medicine.

As Shelbydog ages, I have been making plans for the disposition of her body. As a servant of God, her remains deserve respect; they housed God's Spirit. My first plan was to bury her body in my back yard, but I thought about who would respect her grave after I'm dead and my executor sells my lot and home. Even if her grave were marked, would the future owners treat her final resting place with respect? Thus, I contacted a pet cemetery. I had hoped to purchase a pre-need contract, but the cemetery director did not offer that service. Even though the director favored cremation over burial, I got an estimate on how much it would cost to bury Shelby in a pet cemetery, where her grave would be marked, respected, and honored by those who knew her. While doing some online research, I was amazed at the variety of burial caskets and blankets for dogs; such things are designed to show respect and honor the deceased pet.

When researching pet cemeteries, I also came across a Dog's Last Will and Testament. It was prepared by a canine's owner before the dog had to be euthanized due to a cancerous tumor. While the reading of the Dog's Last Will and Testament made me sad, it also got me thinking about Shelby's Last Will and Testament. Since Shelby spent the fifth year of her life in animal shelters, I'm sure she would want her food bowls, water bowls, toys, bed, blankets, coats, bandanas, towels, leashes, harnesses, shoulder brace, and leftover food and medicines to go to a local animal shelter. Thinking about all this made me sad; I went to Shelby and petted, hugged, and kissed her, telling her, "I love you," over and over again. When the time comes, I will respect both her body and her wishes—as well as I can determine them—and I will pray that her spirit will be united intimately with Spirit, whose divine manifestation she was and is.

I am deeply affected by Shelby's aging; my companion gets older day by day before my eyes. I think I am pre-grieving her death, even though I hope it will not come soon. Because I love her, I want to keep her with me for as long as I can. And yet, I do not want her to be living and suffering just because I cannot let her go. I cannot own Shelby; she is a free spirit entrusted by God to my care.

Because both of us are already in God, both of us mediate the divine presence to each other. She is my burning bush; her red highlights flash the divine presence, especially when she is in sunshine. I am consoled by the belief that we will not go out of existence; we will be changed, transformed—not ended—when we die. The love we share now will continue on the other side of the grave. I know her death will leave me feeling empty, because she so fills me with grace now. I love her, because I've gotten to know her and trust her. She is my shadow, because she knows me well. She knows how to lead me across the street, when that is what she wants to do. She knows how to pester me to put more chicken on her food by refusing to eat what is in her bowls. She knows how to solicit a bellyrub from me, when I go into the bedroom and find her lying awake in her bed and ready to take her on a walk. She knows to lie by my chair when I am eating dinner and gaze at me with her big brown eyes until she gets a bite of food off my plate. Even though I tell her that she cannot have any food off my plate, she always manages to coax a bite from my hand! Shelby is a spiritual dog!

Reflection Questions

1. What is your understanding of spirituality? How do you apply it to your pet?

2. How are you and your pet connected spiritually?

3. What are your plans for the disposition of your pet's body after his or her death?

21

Thunder and Lightning

E VER SINCE SHELBYDOG CAME to live with me, she has been afraid of thunder and lighting. As soon as thunder was heard, she would find me and lie close by me or she would head to her bed to hide. If I were in the living room, she would leave her front porch room and lie on a rug near me. Sometimes I would cover her with a blanket, and she would fall asleep. At other times, I would invite her to go with me to the front porch; she would sit facing the glass door and I would kneel behind her with my arms around her. I would tell her, "Nothing is going to hurt you," while we listened to the thunder, saw the flashes of lightning, watched the wind bend the tree branches, and observed the rain falling on the driveway. Once the thunder, lightning, and rain stopped, she was OK to be alone again.

After repeating the above process over the course of three years, I was ready to accept the fact that Shelby was not going to get over her fear of thunder and lightning. She continued to find me, sit or lie near me, and find security. Then, she began to leave my security and return to her front porch room and listen to the thunder and watch the lightning and the rain. I would follow her and tell her, "Nothing is going to hurt you." In the spring of 2023, she began to awaken me during the night when she heard thunder or saw lightning flashes in the window. She would sit on the rug facing the door, the usual sign that she wanted to go outside. However, when I opened the bedroom door, she headed through the house to the front door. After I opened it, she went onto the front porch and sat in front of the glass door and listened to the thunder and watched the lightning and rain. She turned around to look at me and beckoned me to go and kneel behind her and join her. And so I did. I came to the realization that she was no longer afraid of thunder and lightning.

In fact, she was using the occasion of thunder and lightning to draw us closer together. She had come to understand that thunder and lightning were not going to hurt her. And she wanted to imitate the practice I had initiated, namely sitting on the front porch and watching the lightning and listening to the thunder. There are still occasions when she fears the thunder and lightning, especially when the thunder is very loud and there are many lightning flashes across the dark sky. All we have to do is go to the front porch and sit together watching nature's show. I still tell her, "Nothing is going to hurt you." With me at her side, she relaxes and watches and listens as nature puts on her light show complete with musical accompaniment.

Reflection Questions

1. Is your pet afraid of thunder and/or lightning? Explain.

2. When it is thundering and/or lightning, what practice might you initiate to bring you and your pet closer together? Explain.

3. Is your pet afraid of fireworks? Explain.

22

Happy

I N GENERAL, SHELBY IS a happy dog. When she is happy, her brown eyes are fully open, her ears may be raised or lying on her head, her tail is raised and pointed over her back to her head, and she is very excited, often not being able to be still. After taking her to the back yard, she goes to her favorite places, pees, then runs through the yard on the labyrinth of walkways through the gardens, into the garage, into the house, and up the stairs into the kitchen and through the house to the front porch!

I know she is happy when she displays a big smile on her face. While taking a walk, she demonstrates how happy she is by throwing herself onto green grass and rolling and rolling, running, and playing. After placing herself in the grass, she rolls from side to side. Then, she stops on her back, and with all four feet in the air, twists her head and neck to wiggle her body. All the while, she makes hah, hah breathing sounds. After she stops wiggling, she rolls onto her side, gets up on all four feet, shakes herself from nose to tail, and continues the walk. In the house, I know she wants to play, when she brings me one of her toys and invites me to follow her to wherever she is headed. She drops the toy and rolls onto her back, wanting a bellyrub. She is happy.

The sunshine makes Shelbdog happy. She loves to spend her morning lying in the sunshine, moving when she gets too warm, getting a drink of water, and going back to the sunshine streaming through the glass door.

After discovering that she had some joint inflammation and giving her doses of Carprofen prescribed by her vet to counter it, she was very happy. She slept better throughout the night, and she trotted and ran on walks. I didn't know how much pain she was in; the previous Shelbydog returned. She began to paw me to follow her to a rug, where she solicited bellyrubs. She was excited to walk, trot, and run again, except in the heat and humidity.

Shelby is happy when she is lying on the front porch and her tail is wagging against the door or the floor. She is happy when she is lying on a rug, all crouched and ready to spring into action. She is happy when she comes to the dining room ready to eat a meal or to get a bone. When her behavior, especially tail wagging, demonstrates happiness, I know she is not in pain.

She demonstrates happiness when she plays with her pillow on the living room floor. With lots of heavy breathing, she rolls the pillow under her until she pushes it aside, then goes to it and repeats the fun. She demonstrates happiness bringing either duckie or dearie to anyone who comes to the front door. When Shelby is happy, I am happy.

Shelbydog is happy going on a hike; she likes to be first on the trail, leading the way. When crossing a creek or river, she gets very happy when she can get into the cold water and submerse herself, except for her head, and emerge quickly from the stream and shake the water from her coat, spraying anyone near her!

While getting a bath did not make her happy in the past, it does so today. When I call her to come into the bathroom to get her bath, she responds excitedly by entering the room and sitting in front of the walk-in shower. She enjoys getting wet, shampooed, and rinsed, but her favorite part is getting dried with a large towel. She smiles as I rub the towel all over her. Once she is somewhat dry, she runs through the house to lie in the sunshine. She is so happy that she can barely contain herself! I usually follow her to the front porch, roll her on her back, and towel her belly and legs. She responds by smiling and rolling from side to side. I tell her how good she smells after drying her. It is easier to give her a bath if I start talking about it five to seven days before it is going to occur. When I mention the bath on the day it is to occur, she often goes to the bathroom and waits for me to get rugs and towels to be ready. It makes her happy for the rest of the day, especially when she gets a clean harness and bandana.

Shelby demonstrates happiness when she is permitted to enter a store, like a hardware store, a trinket store, or an art shop. She gets to walk with me through the aisles and smell things. Usually, she gets petted and a treat from a store clerk at checkout.

Shelby is happy when she cleans her favorite toy: duckie. She licks duckie from bill to tail, the way she would lick a puppy. She has had duckie for years, but never torn him. She is also happy when she gets a cloth bone; she looks for the threads, where it was sewed together. Finding the threads, she pulls them out until the opening on the bone is large enough for her to get her teeth around the stuffing, which she removes piece by piece and piles on either side of her head. Her goal is to find the plastic squeaky inside and remove it. Finding the toy that makes the noise makes Shelby happy.

Shelby is happy when she visits her friends or they visit her. When her friends are around, she spends a lot of time with them soliciting pettings and bellyrubs, as they talk to her. She is happy when they take her for a walk.

Shelby is happy when the weather is cool. She likes to trot and run in the cool breeze. Before he died, she used to try to get Hutch, a neighborhood dog, to run and play with her, but he just stood still and wouldn't move. She'd even find a stick and tempt him to take it away from her. Chewing on a stick makes her happy. In the cold, she trots and runs until she gets warm and her tongue hangs out of her mouth. She will stop to smell something along the sidewalk, road, or trail and, then, suddenly take off like a rocket to the next stop. She is happy, like she is young again!

Smelling, walking, trotting, and running through leaves makes Shelby happy. Her tail is curled up and pointed towards her head, as she rushes through the leaves, especially those piled by neighbors in their yards.

Shelby demonstrates her happiness to see me after I have been gone to the grocery store or to keep an appointment by meeting me at the back door with one of her toys in her mouth. As I come in the door, she runs up the steps and through the house, tempting me to follow her. Sometimes, she backtracks to be sure that I see her carrying her toy. Once I catch her, I calm her and pet her. She demonstrates her happiness by licking my hand.

Reflection Question

1. How do you know when your pet is happy? What are the signs? Make a list.

23

Stubborn

A S Shelbydog ages, she becomes more stubborn. That is because she is becoming more secure in being who she truly is. Her stubbornness is demonstrated often on walks. After taking off on our usual walking route, Shelby may suddenly stop at a side street, plant all four feet firmly on the ground, concrete, or asphalt and refuse to move. She has decided that she does not want to walk any farther; in other words, she is ready to head home. The only way to get her moving again is to hold the leash tightly and point my body in the direction we need to continue walking! After a few minutes she determines that I am going to prevail, and she begins to walk the usual way again. However, there are times when she keeps crossing the street from one side to another; there is little I can do to keep her from moving from one side to the other.

In the autumn, winter, and early spring months, as she passes by me to go to bed, I'll often call her to come and get a bellyrub. She will not come. She acts like she didn't hear me, and she continues on to her bed in the bedroom.

If the day is cloudy, or if it has rained during the day, Shelby will not walk but a block or two. I don't know if there is any connection to the lack of sunshine and wet pavement. She stops with all four feet firmly anchored and makes clear at the next intersection that she will go no farther except home. Once home, a visit to the back yard is OK.

Shelby's stubbornness is also manifested in the strategies she has developed for slowing down on walks. Sometimes, she stops and lies on the grass. Coaxing her to get up and keep moving does not motivate her. All that can be done is wait until she is ready to continue the walk. She gets up and begins to walk in the same direction we were going.

Her stubbornness comes through on her moody days, when she is very uncooperative. On those days, she stops over and over again for no apparent reason. She stops and rolls, stops and rolls, stops and rolls. She may snap at another dog, if one is near. I find myself often having to pull her home, and I feel so bad later that I apologize to her.

Stubbornness is displayed when she stops suddenly in the middle of the street we are crossing and usually changes her mind about crossing to the other side. When she does not get her way, she is very undesirable.

Until recent times, Shelby was very stubborn on bath days. At first, she wouldn't come to the bathroom when called; I'd have to go get her and lead her with her harness to the bathroom. Then, I'd have to lift her into the shower, remove the harness, and proceed to engage in a wrestling match, as I got her wet, shampooed her, rinsed her, and dried her. Over the course of the years, she has become more cooperative on bath days.

For some reason on some days Shelby stubbornly refuses to eat her meals, especially breakfast and dinner, both of which have her medicines wrapped in soft dog food in her bowl. No amount of coaching will get her to eat. I've tried giving her treats first instead of after the meal. I've tried putting something tasty on her food. What works is boiled chicken breast; all it takes are a few pieces torn into strips and placed on top of the food in her bowl. When she is in a stubborn mood, she wants to eat spread eagle on the floor; I put her bowl of food between her extended front paws, and she will, usually, eat some of her food. However, there are times when she moves away, leaving the bowl of food where I put it.

When she is in one of her stubborn moods, she will not take her medicine. She will not take it in her food. She will not take it wrapped in soft dog food in a small bowl that I hold near her nose. She will raise her head as far back as she can, or she will turn it from side to side, as I try to get her to take the medicine I have in a small bowl.

As Shelby gets older and older, she also gets more and more stubborn about many things. There are times when I call her—and I know she hears me—and she refuses to come.

Reflection Questions

1. When is your pet stubborn?

2. What is the cause of your pet's stubbornness, as best as you can determine?

24
Nap

I F I DECIDE TO take a nap after lunch or mid-afternoon on my bed, Shelby will often come and take a nap on her bed. Of course, she naps frequently during the day in her room on the front porch. If I am not feeling well and lie on my bed at any time of the day, Shelby will usually join me on her bed, which is next to mine. Sometimes she stays for as long as I stay, and at other times she gets up and walks to the front porch, after she is sure that I am OK.

When we are in Colorado, an afternoon nap is part of our daily schedule. While I stretch out on the futon or sofa, Shelby curls in her overstuffed chair. Before I fall asleep, I hear Shelby snoring! Those afternoon Colorado naps last about an hour.

If she is very tired, Shelby will often go to her bed at home and take a nap in the afternoon. If she hears me getting ready to shower in the afternoon, I see her going to her bed for a nap. Often, I cover her with her blanket, like I do at night, and within a few minutes I can hear her snoring! Sometimes her afternoon naps are long, and sometimes they are short.

Reflection Question

1. Where does your pet like to nap? Explain.

25

Left Leg

WHEN SHELBY LIES, SHE has a tendency to bend her left foot under her. One time when she was playing with her dog friend, Conan, a Labrador retriever, she stopped to rest with her left foot under her. He, being much larger than she, pounced in play on her. His weight caused a sprain in her left foot, and she cried in pain. I got strips of cloth and wrapped her foot in them, and that enabled her to walk around the house with little pain. I also bought her a foot brace, which she wore for several weeks every time we went outside for a walk. In time, the left food healed.

However, a year or so later, while on a walk, either she slipped into a hole or stepped on something—with her left foot—which caused her to squeal and lift her foot in the air. I tried examining the foot, thinking that she had stepped on something or had something stuck between her toes, but I couldn't find anything. While bending the foot a little, she barked and cried a little. I made her lie on her side in the grass so I could better examine her paw. I could find nothing. Since she couldn't walk home, I got a neighbor to watch her, while I went and got the car to pick up Shelby and take her home. She hobbled to the car, I took her home, and put the foot brace on her. That enabled her to put her weight on that foot in the house. Within a day, she was walking on her left foot, but I kept the brace on it for a week, when we took short walks outside.

From that experience, I again realized that Shelby's pain caused me great distress, because I wasn't sure what I needed to do to remove it. Besides using the foot brace, I prayed for her healing, for divine intervention to heal a servant of God. Because I love her so much, I cannot stand to see her suffer in light of all the suffering she has already endured. I prayed that God would have mercy on his servant, Shelbydog, and he did. The next morning, her foot was much better; we were able to walk a square block. She wore her foot brace all day. I thanked God for healing her so quickly. A couple of days later, she was trotting again, while still wearing her brace. Within five days, while still wearing the brace, we walked a mile.

A week later, while still wearing her foot brace, we walked by the home of two friends, one of whom is a veterinarian. He asked about the foot brace, and I explained what had happened a week before. The vet said that Shelby might have some arthritis in her left foot and leg. That got me thinking about how I had noticed her slowing down a lot on our walks. So, I went online and read about dog arthritis. Then, I called Shelby's vet and scheduled an appointment.

Neighbors noted that Shelby had a slight limp on her left side, when they saw us walking. The two times that she had sprained that foot was most likely the cause. As she aged, the limp kept getting worse; she was lumbering. I began to put on the foot brace on her left foot, when we went for walks. And that helped alleviate some of the limp.

After keeping our appointment with her veterinarian, I learned that she had some joint inflammation and may have been in pain. The vet devised a plan, which consisted of two-weeks on an anti-inflammatory drug followed by a daily joint-restorative chew. I saw results from the anti-inflammatory drug the next morning; she was trotting, running, and feeling better. She was smiling. She was happy. And she was sleeping better. Once the joint-restorative chew began, I witnessed the return of my old Shelbydog. Her energy returned, as her pain disappeared. On some days she wanted to walk farther than we went usually. She ate her three daily meals, and she took her medicines. And I could tell that she was feeling much better.

To keep the joint inflammation under control, she continued to take her anti-inflammatory drug once a day. About three months later, I observed her awaken from a nap, stretch, and emit a squeal. I think her left foot was asleep, because she had been sleeping on it or she was having a muscle cramp or spasm. She got out of the overstuffed chair in which she had been napping and lay on the rug and began to lick her left foot. Not long later, she ate her meal and went back to her chair for a nap.

She continued to take her anti-inflammatory medicine daily along with her joint-restorative chew daily throughout the next year. While there was a very light limp on her left side, it did not seem to bother her until a year later. On a morning walk I noticed that the limp was more pronounced than it had been before. I theorized that she had been running up and down steps and jumping in and out of the car often, and those could have been affecting her left leg. A couple of days later, the limp was gone. She was trotting and running again on our walks.

Of course, Shelby was aging, and all was well until six months later. I noticed that bending her left foot to take off her harness in the evening seemed to cause her pain. Her left leg was stiff, and she didn't like having to bend it a little to get the harness off. I also noticed that she was limping again and stumbling on the steps. I tried putting her foot brace on again, and I began to give her two daily doses of her anti-inflamatory medicine. However, he left leg continued to be stiff when I took off her harness. Nevertheless, the daily double dose of her anti-inflammatory medicine removed her pain, as she was back to trotting and running on walks.

My goal was pain management for Shelbydog, while keeping her active. Her vet had told me that I needed to keep her moving. By mid-July 2023, her limp got worse, and on a morning walk she was struggling to move. I e-mailed her vet, who prescribed a pain pill for her, when she needed it. I also went online and researched shoulder braces for dogs. I found single shoulder braces and double shoulder braces; I ordered her a double shoulder brace. After it arrived, I read the directions about how to put it on Shelbydog. Because she likes to wear things, she sat still while I figured out how to get her legs into the leggings and get the strap from the right legging across her back and through the buckle on the left legging and then tighten it. Our first walk with it was short, as Shelby adjusted to wearing it. The second walk with it found her adjusting to both the way it helped her and the ways it limited her. By the third walk, she was letting it help her. She trotted and ran with it. Gradually, we increased the distance we walked, and Shelby felt better, trotting and running. I was very proud of her. Her limp was decreased with the use of the brace, which kept her shoulders, and, therefore, her front legs and feet, lined correctly. She began to stop and roll on her back and wiggle with her brace. While it makes her hot because of the elastic strap over her back connecting the shoulders of her front legs, it aids her walking and going up and down steps. It does limit how far up she can jump. She wears the brace all day; I remove it after we have finished our evening walk.

Reflection Questions

1. With what physical issues of your pet have you dealt? Make a list and indicate what you did when faced with each physical issue?

2. How does knowing that your pet may be in pain make you feel?

26

Rascal

A RASCAL IS A MISCHIEVOUS animal. Shelbydog is a rascal. When she came to live with me, she was scared of vacuum cleaners. Now that she has learned that the vacuum will not hurt her, she is fascinated by it. When I am running it over rugs, she gets as close as she can to it, even sitting on the rug I am attempting to vacuum. I make her move so that I can finish vacuuming a rug!

Cloudy days and rainy days used to make her restless; I think they depressed her. So, after reading about the effect a light lamp can have on people, I bought her such a lamp. On cloudy and rainy days I turn it on, and Shelby lies under it, as if it were the sun shining through the door on the front porch. It moderates her mood, making her happy. On dreary days without sunshine, she spends the morning lying under it.

In her first book, Shelby narrates how she found some leftover chicken on a plate, which had been placed on a low counter, in the house we stay in my hometown. All in the house learned not to leave any food on that low counter when Shelby was around; she was able to get it, eat it, and end up with diarrhea. On another occasion, we were eating rotisserie chicken for dinner. I had carved it on a platter, but I had placed the platter on a high counter. While we were eating, Shelby sneaked into the kitchen and jumped to the high counter. When she placed her front paws on the counter, they caught the edge of the platter, causing it and the chicken on it to flip off onto the floor. The loud noise of a platter crashing to the floor got those eating dinner to rise from their chairs and head to the kitchen, where they found pieces of chicken all over the floor and hundreds of pieces of platter covering most of the floor. Hearing the loud noise she had made, Shelby left the kitchen and headed to the dining room, passing all others headed to the kitchen. I got a broom and began to sweep up pieces of platter after picking up the chicken, which still had its skin on it. Another person got a mop with hot water and soap and began to mop the floor where I had swept. Then, both of us searched for shards of platter under cabinets, the cooking stove, and other places in the kitchen where they came to rest. After finishing dinner, I skinned the chicken and made it ready to be used in chicken salad the next day. Shelby got into a little trouble, although she was more scared of the noise the platter had made crashing to the floor!

When we are in Colorado, we stay in an apartment over a three-car garage. A stairway leads to the apartment door with a small porch or landing in front of the door. The first time Shelby wanted to sit in the sun on the porch, I went to check on her and found her gone, even though I had told her that she was not permitted to go down the steps. I called her, came inside and looked for her—thinking that she had come in without me seeing her—and went back outside and down the steps to find her at the bottom of the steps. I called her to follow me to the porch. A while later, while she was still in the sun on the porch, I went out to check on her again, only to see her trotting down the lane. In a loud voice, I called her to come back, and she did so slowly and reluctantly. After that I began to tie her on the porch with her leash. Ultimately, she learned that she had porch privileges, but she could not walk down the steps.

Because the apartment was a new place to stay, Shelby did not like being left alone. She demonstrated that by taking all the pillows off the futon and throwing them onto the floor. Because she scratched the pillows onto the floor, she got her toe nails caught in the some of the futon coverings' threads and ripped open a spot, which I was able to repair with a piece of fabric from the apartment owner.

After leaving Shelby alone in the two-story house in which we stay, when in my hometown, she went through the whole house and took all the pillows off of couches, chairs, and beds on both the first and second floors and left them on the floor. It is her form of protesting being left alone or left behind.

On recycling days, I fill the back of the Jeep with boxes of items to be taken to the recycling center and dumped into the huge bins. Shelby always goes along, but she cannot sit in the back seat because it is lowered to make room for the boxes of recyclables. Thus, she has to sit in the passenger seat.

Instead of lying in the seat, she prefers to sit like a co-driver or co-pilot. She turns her head from right to left looking at other cars, trees, and people. When making turns, I reach over and grab her harness to hold onto her and keep her from sliding off the seat onto the car floor. Over the course of repeated trips to the recycling center, she has learned to use her toes to keep her balance and not slide off the seat!

On laundry day, when I am changing the linens on my bed, she likes to sneak up behind me and rub one of her front paws on the back of one of my legs. Once she has my attention, she turns around and runs through the house to the front porch. She wants me to follow her there, where she lies on her back awaiting a bellyrub. If I do not follow her immediately, she repeats her moves over and over until I do follow her.

On walks in the autumn, she likes to find piles of leaves and throw herself into them and roll and roll and wiggle and wiggle around in them. In the spring and summer, she does the same when finding patches of green grass.

Shelby demonstrates her rascality, when she sneaks to the basement and tears a rug that lies on the floor. I can never catch her doing it, but she embeds her toe nails in the fibers of the rug and pulls out the threads, leaving parts of the rug in shreds.

In 2022, I bought Shelbydog three interactive toys. The first was a ball. After putting kibble in it, I rolled it around the floor before her to demonstrate how to get the kibble out of it. She liked eating the kibble that came out of it, as I rolled it around the floor. However, after I showed her how to roll it with her feet, she refused to enter the process. As long as I rolled the ball and the kibble came out, she was happy to eat the kibble, but she would not play with it. Ultimately, I put it away.

The second toy consisted of a square with latches to slide open or domes to slide off to discover kibble under the latch or dome. I showed her how to slide the latches and domes with her foot, but she preferred to use her tongue. I got her to open all the latches and domes one time. Then, being the rascal she is, she didn't want to play with it again. Like the first toy, I put it away.

The third toy was a larger version of the second one. The series of sliding latches required the movement of one in order to move another. As in previous times, I showed her how to move the latches with her foot in order to find kibble. She wasn't interested. So, I picked it up and put it away.

I know she was capable of mastering all three interactive toys; she preferred the role of rascal.

She also shows herself to be a rascal on what I call "rolling days." A rolling day is one in which she stops repeatedly during walks to throw herself onto a pile of leaves, a patch of grass, on the asphalt, or on the bare ground two or three times and roll and roll and roll and roll. On a rolling day, it is common to find her on the living room rug rolling back and forth several times during the day. It is also common to find her rolling on the tile floors. The rolling days demonstrate what a rascal Shelbydog is.

Reflection Questions

1. In what specific ways is your pet a rascal? Make a list.

2. What criteria are you using to determine your pet's rascality?

27

Songs, a Poem, and an Acrostic

O VER THE COURSE OF the years, I have written songs about Shelbydog set to the tune of another popular song. The first one, *Shelbydog, Shelbydog*, below is set to the tune of the old *Robinhood* TV show theme song. The second, *Shelbydog Song* is set to the tune of *O Christmas Tree*, also known as *O Tannenbaum*!

Shelbydog, Shelbydog

1. Shelbydog, Shelbydog, running through the field;
Shelbydog, Shelbydog, never will she yield.
Feared by the bad, Loved by the good,
Shelbydog, Shelbydog!

2. Shelbydog, Shelbydog, going for a walk.
Shelbydog, Shelbydog, Oh! If she could talk?
Feared by the bad, Loved by the good,
Shelbydog, Shelbydog!

3. Shelbydog, Shelbydog, eating her white rice.
Shelbydog, Shelbydog, she is quite nice.
Feared by the bad, Loved by the good,
Shelbydog, Shelbydog!

4. Shelbydog, Shelbydog, nose in the grass!
Shelbydog, Shelbydog, she can be crass.
Feared by the bad, Loved by the good,
Shelbydog, Shelbydog!

5. Shelbydog, Shelbydog, nose in the leaves.
Shelbydog, Shelbydog, doing what she please.
Feared by the bad, Loved by the good,
Shelbydog, Shelbydog!

6. Shelbydog, Shelbydog, lying in the sun.
Shelbydog, Shelbydog, she is having fun.
Feared by the bad, Loved by the good,
Shelbydog, Shelbydog!

7. Shelbydog, Shelbydog, brindle color brown.
Shelbydog, Shelbydog, often with a frown.
Feared by the bad, Loved by the good,
Shelbydog, Shelbydog!

Shelbydog Song

(Tune: O Christmas Tree [O Tannenbaum!])
1. O Shelbydog, O Shelbydog,
How brindle is your color!
O Shelbydog, O Shelbydog,
How brindle is your color!

2. In the sun you sparkle red
And while you lie upon your bed.
O Shelbydog, O Shelbydog,
How brindle is your color!

3. You savor a long bellyrub
But hate indeed the bathing tub.
O Shelbydog, O Shelbydog,
How brindle is your color!

4. You are picky with your food
And very often in your mood.
O Shelbydog, O Shelbydog,
How brindle is your color!

5. Cheese it is morn, noon, and night,
While cats and squirrels you afright.
O Shelbydog, O Shelbydog,
How brindle is your color!

6. Your bones are strewn from room to room
And you gaze upon the moon.
O Shelbydog, O Shelbydog,
How brindle is your color!

7. We bask in joy with all your love
You manifest from up above.
O Shelbydog, O Shelbydog,
How brindle is your color!

8. What grace descends to us below
From God who made you just so-so.
O Shelbydog, O Shelbydog,
How brindle is your color!

Shelbydog

my sixty-pound brindle friend asleep snores
with paws tucked in front and head on chair's arm
in mountain sunshine brindle red streaks soar
her very brown eyes and small smiling face charm

cat-chasing dream into running she pours
sixteen toes with long nails hear her alarm
eye lids raise reality in time bores
quiet breaking blanketed body warms

seventy-three years dog's open mouth roars
indeed servant of God does no harm
my companion four-legged friend asleep snores
with paws tucked in front and head on chair's arm

Shelby Acrostic by Jenson Kimmons

S = Surprising
H = Helper
E = Exciting
L = Loving
B = Beautiful
Y = Your Best Friend

Reflection Questions

1. If you wrote a song about your pet, what would it say? To what tune would you set it?

2. If you wrote a poem about your pet, what would it say?

3. Using your pet's name, prepare an acrostic.

Bibliography

Nuttall, Mark. "Siberia and the Arctic." In *World Mythology*, edited by Arthur Cottrell, 130–39. Bath, UK: Paragon, 2003.

Recent Books by Mark G. Boyer
published by Wipf & Stock

Nature Spirituality: Praying with Wind, Water, Earth, Fire

A Spirituality of Ageing

Weekday Saints: Reflections on Their Scriptures

Human Wholeness: A Spirituality of Relationship

A Simple Systematic Mariology

Praying Your Way through Luke's Gospel and the Acts of the Apostles

An Abecedarian of Animal Spirit Guides: Spiritual Growth through Reflections on Creatures

Overcome with Paschal Joy: Chanting through Lent and Easter—Daily Reflections with Familiar Hymns

Taking Leave of Your Home: Moving in the Peace of Christ

An Abecedarian of Sacred Trees: Spiritual Growth through Reflections on Woody Plants

Divine Presence: Elements of Biblical Theophanies

Fruit of the Vine: A Biblical Spirituality of Wine

Names for Jesus: Reflections for Advent and Christmas

Talk to God and Listen to the Casual Reply: Experiencing the Spirituality of John Denver

Christ Our Passover Has Been Sacrificed: A Guide through Paschal Mystery Spirituality—Mystical Theology in The Roman Missal

Rosary Primer: The Prayers, The Mysteries, and the New Testament

From Contemplation to Action: The Spiritual Process of Divine Discernment Using Elijah and Elisha as Models

Love Addict

All Things Mary: Honoring the Mother of God—An Anthology of Marian Reflections

Shhh! The Sound of Sheer Silence: A Biblical Spirituality that Transforms

What is Born of the Spirit is Spirit: A Biblical Spirituality of Spirit

Very Short Reflections—for Advent and Christmas, Lent and Easter, Ordinary Time, and Saints—through the Liturgical Year

Living Parables: Today's Versions

My Life of Ministry, Writing, Teaching, and Traveling: The Autobiography of an Old Mines Missionary

300 Years of the French in Old Mines: A Narrative History of the Oldest Village in Missouri

Journey into God: Spiritual Reflections for Travelers

Monthly Entries for the Spiritual but not Religious through the Year: Texts, Reflections, Journal/Meditations, and Prayers for the Spiritual but not Religious

The Shelbydog Chronicles by Shelby Cole as Recorded by Mark G. Boyer: A Novel

Four Catholic Pioneers in Missouri: Lamarque, Kenrick, Fox, and Hogan: Irish Missionaries and Their Supporter

Smothered with Inexhaustible Mercy: An Anthology of Poems

Spirituality for the Solitary: A Handbook for Those Who Live Alone

Seasons of Biblical Spirituality: Spring, Summer, Autumn, and Winter

Biblical Names for God: An Abecedarian Anthology of Spiritual Reflections for Anytime

www.ingramcontent.com/pod-product-compliance
Lightning Source LLC
Chambersburg PA
CBHW060436260626
47161CB00005B/1952